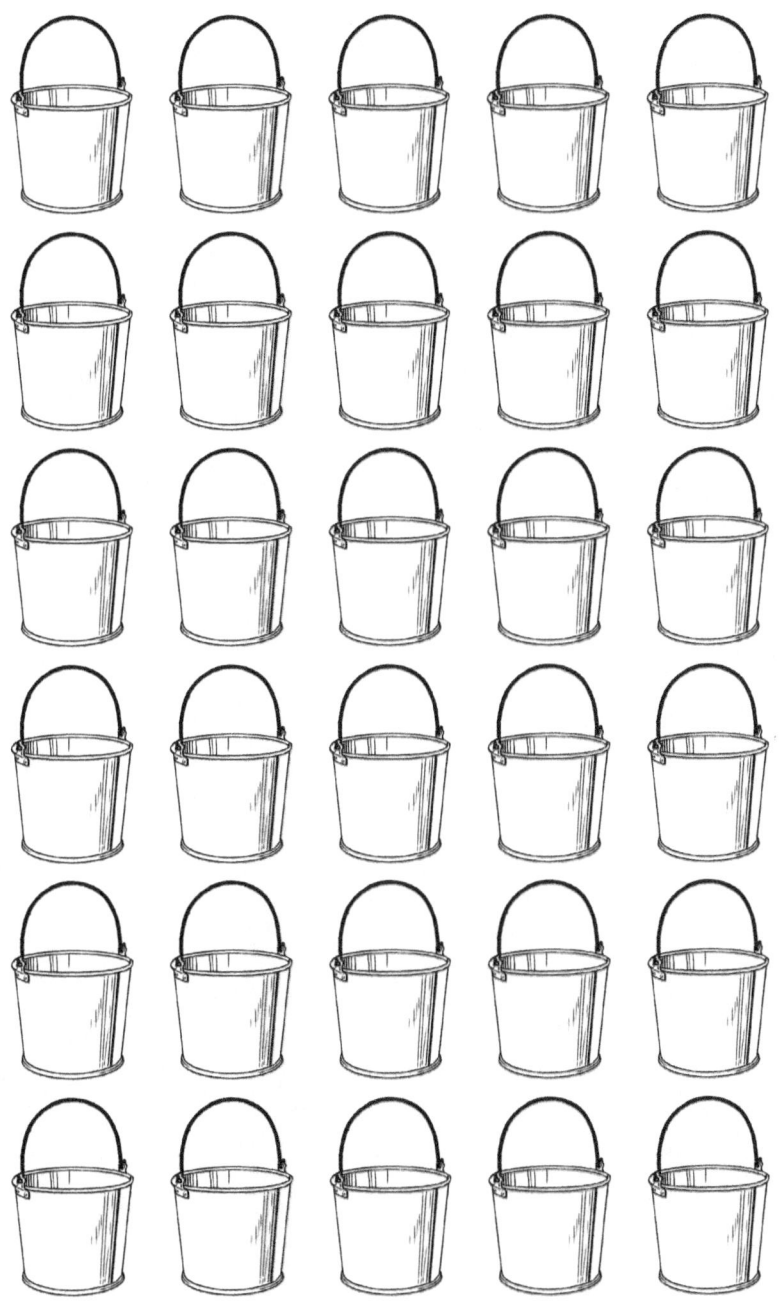

Pure Slush Books

2014
May

Vol. 5

a Pure Slush book

Pure Slush

2014 May Vol. 5 is edited by Matt Potter and published by Pure Slush, February 2014.

Cover photograph copyright © Leonardo Barbosa
http://www.leonardobarbosa.net
statue in Piazza Navona, Rome, Italy

ISBN: 978-1-925101-30-0

You can find *Pure Slush* at http://pureslush.webs.com

Copies of all *Pure Slush* publications can be bought
at http://pureslush.webs.com/store.htm

All queries re *Pure Slush* can be made
via email to edpureslush@live.com.au

A note on differences in punctuation and spelling

Pure Slush proudly features (both online and in print) writers from all over the English-speaking world. Some speak and write English as their first language, while for others, it's their second or third or even fourth language. Naturally, across all versions of English, there are differences in punctuation and spelling, and even in meaning. These differences are reflected in the stories *Pure Slush* publishes, and it accounts for any differences in punctuation, spelling and meaning found within these pages.

stories by

Guilie Castillo-Oriard

Townsend Walker

Derek Osborne

Gloria Garfunkel

John Wentworth Chapin

Lynn Beighley

Andrew Stancek

Rachel Ambrose

Gill Hoffs

Susan Tepper

Jessica McHugh

Shane Simmons

Michelle Elvy

Len Kuntz

Michael Webb

James Claffey

Gwendolyn Joyce Mintz

Stephen V. Ramey

Gay Degani

Sally-Anne Macomber

Mandy Nicol

Margaret Bingel

Darryl Price

Teresa Burns Gunther

Matt Potter

Gary Percesepe

Nathaniel Tower

Kimberlee Smith

Vanessa Weibler Paris

Joanne Jagoda

h. l. nelson

Cause for Celebration

by Guilie Castillo-Oriard

Luis Villalobos sits in a dark hotel room. The lights of Mexico City spread below, precious stones scattered on black velvet. He loves this city, the vibrancy, but up here he's detached from it, insulated from the cacophony of its streets by the thick glass and soundproofed walls of the Nikko Hotel. He'll never be a part of it again, not even when he's down there, in the smog and the crowds and the life. His sinuses haven't stopped aching since they landed. The dry air at twenty-three hundred meters cracks his skin. He walks slower now.

It's been three days. Client meeting after client meeting: breakfasts, lunches, dinners, drinks. A blur of faces and fiscal strategies; of office buildings, security checks, visitor passes; of agendas and proposals and tactful reminders of outstanding invoices. Milena filled up the schedule even today – the Mexican Labor Day – but thanks to his sinus headache he managed to skip the last two meetings. He's been sitting at the window since sunset.

A knock at the door. He closes his eyes, already mourning the solitude he's about to lose.

Knock-knock-knock. One thing Milena won't ever be faulted for is lack of perseverance.

He turns on a light, sets it on low before letting her in. Milena's made-up, dressed-up, and perfumed figure pushes past him. He tries to muster a coat of, if not enthusiasm, at least interest. "How did it go?"

She tosses her handbag and her laptop case on the bed, holds up a Samsonite carry-all with a cocky grin. "They knelt before Zod."

"With offerings?"

She pulls the Samsonite's zipper open like an old-school cabaret stripper and throws him what looks like a very thick checkbook, but isn't. It's a brick of twenty-dollar bills. A Banamex paper strip cinches it around the middle. The bills aren't pristine, but still crisp. A little waxy with the trace of pecuniary fingers.

Milena sits on the bed. "It's only twenty-six K, not even half of what they owe. But it's a start. And they promised –"

"They gave you *cash*?"

"I know, it's inconvenient. But they prefer to avoid a paper trail." She nudges off one black pump, then the other. The soles are bright red. They make Luis think of geishas.

"Milena, we're not dealing meth here. It's our invoices. Corporate directorship, company management. Everything's above –"

"Above board?" She stretches back, reaches for a pillow. "For us, maybe. Not for them. You read the Mexican Fiscal Code lately? Tax planning is a dirty, dirty word."

"Not tax planning. Tax evasion. That's not what we do."

"I love it when you play naive." She folds her arms behind her head, purportedly to prop her up and meet his gaze. She'll have him believe the added bonus of her breasts rising to their best angle is purely coincidental. Her tailored skirt rides up her thighs. The light plays off the sheer pantyhose, highlights the curve of her knee, her calves. But it's the places that remain in shadow that tantalize the most.

Luis feels a tingle of pressure at the base of his penis. He turns back to the window. "Cash isn't just inconvenient. What, you're going to pack it in your suitcase and declare it

14

at the airport? Wouldn't that defeat the whole avoid-a-paper-trail?"

Not long ago he found her husky laughter sexy. Now it sounds childish; petulant, mocking. "Pack it, yes. Declare it, no. And it's not me, honey. It's *we*."

He presses a thumb to his left cheekbone, against the pain building in his sinus cavity. "Even if we split it, we'll be carrying more than ten grand each. We have to declare it."

"You're right." She flings herself off the bed to the minibar, whips out a bottle of Victoria beer. "I'll call the client up now, tell them I can't accept their payment because the mighty Luis Villalobos's moral compass is offended by the notion of cash as yet un-sanitized by the alchemy of bank transactions." She slams the fridge door. Its contents clang dangerously inside. "Will that restore your sense of righteousness? The purity of your soul? Or – no, let's just burn the money. Maybe in the bathtub. This is a smoking room, right? The smoke detectors won't know the difference."

"Milena, that's not –"

She skewers the air between them with the unopened bottle. "What's *wrong* with you?"

Milena in blazing fury isn't anything anyone needs to experience too closely. Even though she stands a full head shorter without the pumps, he takes a step backward. "You know we'd have to declare it. It's the law."

"This isn't about the money. You've been acting like a dick since the FATCA project thing."

He can't hold her gaze, so he looks behind her, into the empty room. "You pulled a shitty trick."

"How many times will we have this conversation? I was protecting you. Ensuring the success of –"

"I don't need protecting."

"I omitted those five entities from the FATCA list so the gaps in information wouldn't mar the results." She puts her hand on his chest, backs him up against the window and

15

the darkness beyond. "I know my clients, Luigi. The Solak woman won't give us diddly-squat."

The earnestness in her eyes might've swayed him a month ago, a couple of weeks even. "What if you're wrong?"

"Am I?" She leans against him, a mimicry of seduction. "Show me, then. Show me Pélagie Solak's signed affidavit. Her proof of residency. Oh, that's right. You don't have them. And because you decided to put those entities back in the final report, against my express instructions, instead of getting the kudos you worked so hard for, Ehrlich Fiduciary is on the FATCA non-compliant list."

This is news to Luis, and his righteousness trips over it. "I didn't –"

"See that coming?" Milena's face is devoid of any sarcasm now. Even the anger has dwindled. "I got the email this morning. You accuse me of backstabbing, Luis, but you did the same. And then some. You compromised the entire company."

"Omitting those entities compromised the integrity of the project!"

She turns away, picks up her shoes from the carpet. "That's rich, coming from you. You know why? You don't understand integrity. That virtuous moral code of yours is more full of holes than a golf course taken over by groundhogs. Sex with your boss for personal gain is acceptable, but –"

"It wasn't –"

"– but being loyal to your employer isn't? How do you reconcile that?" She steps into the pumps, fixes her skirt in front of the mirror.

"I've never been disloyal."

"Sshh." She shakes out her hair, finger-brushes it. "Let me tell you about integrity," she says, pinning her hair back up. "It's about staying true to the people that matter. You know who matters? Our clients. So when your boss –

whether you're sleeping with her or not – tells you that excluding a client from an information request by a foreign government is *for the client's own good*, what do you think integrity dictates? That's right. You obey. Because if you don't, you know who will bear the worst of the consequences? Right again. The *client*."

"You just said it was the company that –"

"Ehrlich is in a corner, because you put us there." She picks up her laptop case, slings her handbag over a shoulder. "There's only one way out."

He should've seen it sooner. "We'll have to resign as directors from Pélagie's entities."

"I wonder if you'll still be on a first-name basis with her once she finds out her whole tax structure is at risk of being dissolved, thanks to you." At the door she pauses, but doesn't turn around. "Take the day off tomorrow. Visit your family, or something."

"But we're meeting with –"

"They were my clients long before they were yours. I can handle it."

When Luis eventually moves, it's only to turn the light off. His head feels like a rotten tomato, all squishy and fragile with the beginnings of remorse. He'll have to go back on his word to leave Pélagie alone. He has to explain, sketch out her options, help her any way he can. Maybe she'll even change her mind and sign the – no, careful. If she perceives this as coercion, another play to get her to sign the damn affidavit – her adjective, not his – she'll shut him down. He'll never get to speak to her again.

There in the darkness, with the city that he once called home shimmering below him, he finally admits it. He's not feeling remorse. He should, but how could he? This mess has given him the one unimpeachable excuse to see Pélagie again. Why that feels like a cause for celebration is not really clear, but then so little is right now.

The bottle of Victoria Milena abandoned on the dresser is still cold. Luis uncaps it, a hiss that ends before it starts, and raises it toward the window to toast the night.

La Ronde / Myron and Gloria

by Townsend Walker

United 1479 drops into LAX; Myron looks out the window for the Los Angeles skyline. Not there today; he goes back to his script, working title: *A Nude in the Garden*. Sex and murder; add in the grit of Newark, he's thinking: maybe *Mystic River* redux, a move to the A list, enough money to buy out Gloria (his wife), enough money to marry Annie (his lover).

The driver waits at baggage claim. Myron climbs in the limo, sinks back into the cool air and leather seats, thinks about his entrance, about Gloria. The one broad he's never been comfortable with, even after twenty years. Always suspicious. He's never been able to tell the "good" lie, his patter never sounds "right" to her; she's always looking for the tell-tale slip of paper, listening for the slip of the tongue. This time, he has been careful, especially since Annie spent time in his room. He double-checked his suitcase and attaché.

The limo drives down San Vicente, right onto Carmelina, up to his house at 151: adobe, Spanish tile roof, wooden balconies, walls necklaced by white roses. *Now I know why I don't live in Newark.* Myron wipes his brow, takes the bouquet of yellow tulips he had the driver pick up, opens the front door.

"Gloria, sweetheart baby, I'm home."

"Myron darling, you don't look so good. Newark wear you out? I told you not to go. Not good for your health, change of seasons, I bet you had a cold and never told me, come here, baby."

She cups his head in her hands.

"Let me take care of you, but first, a big fat smooch for my lover boy."

Myron's thinking: *What's happening here? Not only is she making nice, she's looking good too: tanned, trim, above her usual anorexic 95 pounds, some shape even. She have some work done while I was gone? Maybe a little around the eyes and chin and she wants to ease me into how expensive it was.*

Gloria was an actress, still dresses like a star in the fifties (actually, she never starred in anything but supper club productions). Long flowing gowns in fruit colors: strawberry, plum, apricot; her favorite is kiwi. Gold sandals. Her height, about two inches more than Myron; it's a status symbol for him. Only studs can carry off tall women, he tells himself, and anyone else who remarks on it.

"Baby, you look gorgeous. Not just because I haven't seen you for a month, but double drop dead stunning."

She sashays, twirls, and the gown fans out.

"New diet, new trainer, Serge is amazing. Mimi turned me on to him. You should see *her*."

"This guy a Rooski?"

She takes his arm. "Come over here, sit down, honey."

He sits on the sofa and she tucks her legs under her and nuzzles up to him, strokes his chest. He's trying to remember the last time this happened. Maybe the second year they were married. Since then it's been nag, nag, nag.

Gloria turns his face to hers. "Myron baby, you know how all these years I've been on you about other women. Jabbing here, jabbing there. Well, I went to a new shrink and we talked it out. He made me see how wrong I'd been about you. You in the middle of all those dames looking for

20

roles. I can relate, before you came along, of course. How could you help it, you big hunk? But you were good, I never realized it before. Never anything to prove different."

She looks up at him and gives him a long warm kiss.

"And you were so faithful when you were away, called to wake me up in the morning and tuck me in at night. Such a sweetheart."

She stands up and pulls him out of the sofa.

"You've got to be tired from that flight. You take a nap and I'll fix you a nice salad with some white wine, by the pool."

Myron is tired, from the early flight and the night before, with Annie.

Two hours later, Gloria climbs into his bed, minus gown and slippers, and slowly and gently the sleepy Myron wakes and rises. He strolls out to the deck, hair still wet from a shower.

"You'll never believe what I ran into back in Newark. Blast from the past. A hit job."

Gloria turns stern and serious and surly. "You're not going back into that, you promised."

"No way, no way. But this guy I met was telling me about a woman in Manhattan who put out a contract on her husband. Pretty final way of getting a divorce."

Myron jabbers away about how the guy roughs the wife up and loses the kids in the park.

"Enough, enough, you're not writing a script here."

"I even got a description. Franklin Lancaster Cabot III; goes by Frank. Works at Goldman Sachs on West Street, downtown Manhattan. Six foot three, 250 pounds, pasty complexion, he's inside a lot, curly black hair going gray, beak for a nose, Brooks Brothers dresser, loafers with tassels. And Hermes ties, the silly patterned ones. Outside, Prada Aviators, high end sunglasses, blue tint even in the rain."

"You got that down pat."

"Hey, I'm collecting material, that's all."

"He sounds like a real bastard, hope somebody does him in," Gloria sighs, like she doesn't need to hear more of this.

Myron picks up on it. "Great salad, sweetie, and a lovely wine."

"Vermentino, from Liguria. New wine store down in the center. Italian only. Biondivino. Woman who runs it, Ceri, knows her stuff."

Gloria pours out the rest of the wine and takes the plates to the kitchen. Myron stretches out in his chair and nods off again. She comes back out, pats him fondly on the head. "You do need some sleep." And heads upstairs to unpack his bags.

Ten minutes later.

Gloria straddles the supine Myron in his chair; manages it without touching him; leans her lips into his ear. Shouts: "You son of a bitch, bastard pig, son of a bitch, bastard pig."

Myron's body jumps. Before his eyes are open his mouth gapes, "Wha?" and she stuffs a pair of pink lace panties in it.

"Who is the high priced whore? Carine Gilson lingerie? How much you paying her?"

Myron mumbles through the cloth, "I can explain."

"My lawyer will be happy to hear it. And I've done my homework. I know everything you have and I'm getting a piece of 'Naked Corpse' too. Sayonara sweetheart baby, your bags are at the door."

Myron stumbles through the house, grabs his suitcase, throws it in the back seat of the car. Calls Annie. No pick up. Not really expected. *Probably with Joey, bitch.* "Cuddles, you may be seeing me sooner than later. Gloria found some pink lace, not her size. Yeah, and another thing: the guy in New York, 300 pounds, was he?"

Floating

by Derek Osborne

"Hi, Daddy."

"How's my girl today?"

"I'm fine, how are you?"

"Nausea's not as bad."

Max is pushing the button and raising the bed. He's back at Sloan-Kettering.

"Got an *A* on my editing project. And guess what? I've got an internship this summer, right here in town for CBS."

Andi is twenty-one; she'll be graduating NYU film school this month. She looks so much older these days, black leotard, black stretch pants, petite, like her mother was. *Right here in town*, Max is thinking, *this summer*. Time has been playing tricks on him lately, everything moving too fast; sometimes, moving too slowly.

"That's great," he says, "at CBS? How did you manage that?"

"Well, that's the interesting thing. My Prof said they called and asked about three of us."

"And who is *they*?" Max says, though he has a pretty good idea.

"Some dude, Sid something. I wrote it down. And guess what else? It's for *Miami Blue*. Is that the bomb or what?"

Miami Blue is her favorite show; Rebecca's her favorite actress. She and her sisters are big fans. They text whenever it's on. They all flipped when Max got the gig last December down in Miami. He's been dying to tell them, but he and Rebecca are still a well-kept secret, only Eddie and Anja are in the loop. The tabloids are fishing, pot-shots at Rebecca's recent break-up with her long-time boyfriend, rumors about her leaving the show, hints about some *mystery* man. Rebecca says these things happen like children. One day you wake up and find the whole world knows. The telephone rings. It's the doctor saying it's true.

"Sid Markstein?" Max says.

"What are you smiling at?"

Max tries adjusting the bed again. The back is always too high or too low. He's convinced they make all this stuff for people under six feet tall.

"Nothing," he says.

"That's not your *nothing* smile. What are you thinking?"

When did this happen? That's what he's thinking. *When did my little girl become a woman?*

"Did you pull some strings?" she says.

"Not me."

This second round of chemo has been more aggressive, Max feels like shit. He's weak, can't get comfortable, his butt hurts. As always, he's putting on a good show. His hair is a medical marvel. They've given him the same room he had last time so at least there's Hell Gate and the river for diversion. Andi's pulling up a chair and she's moving Kronos, their name for his little blue robot, arranging the tubes and wires. The SAT phone rings.

It's Rebecca.

"It's business," Max says, "Why don't you hit the cafeteria and get us a bite to eat?"

"I'm not hungry."

"You'll be bored."

"No I won't."

Max looks down at the phone. It keeps ringing; a kind of electronic, nautical alarm. Andi grabs it before he can stop her.

"Hun, don't answer that."

"Mr. Perkins' line," she says, pushing the big red button. The speaker is loud, the phone set for the volume needed out on the wind and water. They both hear Rebecca start laughing. In spite of the pain, he's feeling the calm she brings. Rebecca can't stop. It's an infectious laugh.

"May I ask who is calling?" Andi says, making a face.

"Rebecca Vasquez."

"Yeah, right."

"If Mr. Perkins is not available may I please leave a message?"

Max sees his daughter's jaw drop – the accent, the enunciation – the absence of any contractions. Her eyes grow wide and she's looking from him to the phone and back again. *No fucking way,* she mouths.

"Hello?" Rebecca says, "Is anyone there?"

Andi puts the phone to her ear.

"Who is this, really?"

"Oh? Is this Andi?"

"Yes."

"I've heard so much about you."

"I haven't heard a thing about you."

She's looking at her father.

"I'm sorry, Andi. We have had to do things this way. Sometimes it is better."

"Are you really my dad's girlfriend?"

Rebecca starts laughing again. Andi is holding a hand to her forehead, like, I didn't just say that.

"You'll have to ask your father that question," Rebecca says.

"Are you here? Are you coming over?"

Now she's excited.

"What are you doing on Nantucket?" Rebecca says, "I thought you were still in school?"

No, we're here at …"

"Give me the phone," Max says.

She's turning away so Max can't reach. "Are you in New York?"

"No, I'm in LA."

"Give me the phone," Max says, quietly, deliberately, a father telling his daughter. She's taking him in. She's a smart kid; this isn't hard to figure out. Slowly, she hands it over. He takes the phone, meeting his daughter's eyes. *That's right*, his are saying, *she doesn't know*. Andi walks to the window.

"Hi, you're calling early," Max says, still watching his daughter. "Everything alright?"

"Where are you?"

"The city."

"You didn't tell me."

"It all came up last night after we talked. Booking another gig."

Andi looks over; he's never seen this look on her face.

"I'm sorry I let the cat out of the bag," Rebecca says.

"Had to happen sooner or later. You sound a little off?"

"I'm fine. I just wanted to hear your voice."

"What's wrong?"

"Nothing."

"That's not your nothing voice."

Andi looks over again.

"Why don't we talk after dinner?" Max says.

"I can't, I have an appointment."

"What kind of appointment?"

"An appointment, what difference does it make?"

"It sounds like it makes a great deal of difference."

"A *doctor's* appointment."

"What?"

"They make us take a physical twice a year. I do not like doctors."

"Becca, is everything okay?"

"Yes, Max." But he can hear her breathing. "I'm sorry I called."

"Don't ever be sorry for calling."

"Can I speak with Andi again?"

Andi's heard all of it and walks back to the bed. Max hands her the phone.

"Andi, I know this is a lot to take in."

"You have no idea."

"I need you to do me a favor. No one else can know about your father and me. Not yet. We have to keep it that way for a while."

"I understand."

"I can't wait to meet you," Rebecca says.

"Me too."

"Can you give the phone back to your father?"

Max takes the phone and tries to sit up, making it onto one elbow.

"I love you, Max."

"I love you too."

Something is wrong; that much is sure, but he's thinking what's wrong in the room takes priority. Andi's gone back to the window. Max waits for the screen on the phone to go gray.

"You're doing it again," she says, staring down at the river.

"Doing what?"

"Not telling us. What you did with Mom, you're protecting us. How can you lead her on like that?"

"I'm not leading her on," Max says, raising his voice.

"Can't you tell she's in love with you?"

"Andi, it's complicated."

"I'm not a kid anymore."

No, you aren't, Max is thinking. He can't believe what he's hearing: it may as well be Maggie, his wife, standing there by the window.

"Dad, you're dying."

The words push him back down onto the bed. Andi has turned to face him.

"You think I'm stupid? You think we all don't talk about it?"

"I know ..." Max begins.

"You have to tell her."

Her voice is rising.

"You have to tell her soon."

And then she comes at him. It's that voice, that other dimension. She's screaming.

"You have to tell me!"

"Maggie ..." Max says.

There's a commotion out in the hall and Pam charges in, followed by one of the nurses. Max looks back at his wife but it's not Maggie, it's Andi. The nausea's coming.

"What is going on?" Pam says, "I could hear you all the way down by the elevators."

The nurse stands by the door.

"Ask *him,*" Andi says, pointing a finger. The phone rings again. She grabs it up off the nightstand, looks at the screen and shoves it toward Max. "It's your *girlfriend.*"

"I'm coming out," Rebecca says when he answers.

They can all hear it.

"Okay," Max says.

"They're giving me the plane. I'll be there by dinner."

"Rebecca?" Max says.

"Yes, who did you think it was?"

"What about your appointment?"

"I do not need the god damn appointment, I need you. Where are you staying?"

The nurse leaves the room. Andi is closing her eyes and Pam is slowly getting the picture. *Miami Blue* is her favorite, too. The accent, the careful diction, what Max had said that day on the dock, teasing, she looks at the phone like it may be a bomb. They all hear Rebecca crying.

"Becca, whatever it is we'll be fine."

"Will we?"

Andi has opened her eyes.

"What hotel are you staying?"

Max swallows, hard. He's fighting the nausea. Andi walks over and takes his hand. She looks like her mother again, the day she told him the news. *We have to tell the girls.* Max is thinking how nothing ever works out; how there is only the balance – one thing leaves, another returns – he takes a deep breath, feeling the touch of his daughter's hand.

"Sloan-Kettering."

He can barely get out the next words.

"Room 409."

Sunday, 4th May 2014

Hypomania

by Gloria Garfunkel

Flying Ralph here. Today I am driving home from the best haircut ever and the blossoms on the trees make me feel euphoric, sailing through traffic. I love spring. But I don't think it is spring that is causing the elation. I also bought twenty-five shirts at Macy's at the mall on my way home which I don't need, but when I'm manic, I can't make decisions and so I buy everything. Money goes flying out the window. I bought two cars once. Most of the shirts are pretty nice. Some were mediocre but on sale. I also bought a new Mac laptop and iPhone. I'm feeling stupendous. All the traffic lights are green.

I get home and start writing a novel about a Bipolar Quality Assurance Manager. I write a hundred pages and I feel fantastic. With bipolar hypergraphia, you write a lot but the quality isn't necessarily great. Nevertheless, while you are manic you are also grandiose. So I think it could be a bestseller.

Emerald

by John Wentworth Chapin

Just because I love you doesn't mean you're not crazy. Charles usually says this to his friend Stephanie when she complains that everything is going wrong, that the world is conspiring against her. Charles says it, she laughs, and she reassesses her perspective on the whole thing. It's healthy; it's what friends do.

However, he's just said it to his mother at her favorite café, in response to the saga of the balcony-flower-box feud. When her bright green hyacinth buds withered to black sludge before blooming, she took it to a laboratory for analysis, certain a sinister squirt of RoundUp was the culprit. She used to be president of her condo association but was ousted last year, and ever since then the new president and the treasurer – who engineered the coup – have been out for her blood. The lab results were inconclusive, so she is trying to get access to the security footage.

Just because I love you doesn't mean you're not crazy. She stares at him blankly, as though fumbling to unpack his point. Her mouth opens a moment, then clamps shut, and she shakes her head slowly.

"It's my *birthday*," she reminds him gravely. Charles knows; this is the reason for the lunch, after all, because she has opera tickets for tonight and birthday celebrations are only valid on the day of.

She continues, all hurt and staccato. "That's *not* something you *say* to *people*, you *don't* say 'I love you *but*,' you say 'I *love* you' and leave it at *that*." The gravity of her response – the over-the-top *magnitude* – would be a laugh point in a sitcom, but not now.

Charles replays the phrase – *justbecauseIloveyoudoesn-'tmeanyou'renotcrazy* – in search of the elusive word 'but'. Just because he doesn't find it doesn't mean he should say anything. Normally, he would remain silent, but not today. "That's not what it means. And I didn't say 'but'."

"Perhaps you could enlighten me what you *do* mean, then?" She is brittle.

"I guess I should have said, 'If you're nice to the condo board, they'll be nice back.'"

She tosses her napkin to the table and stands up. "I don't know why you are picking a fight with me *on my birthday*," she says, "but I am going to the ladies' room."

He doesn't know why he's picking a fight with her, either. Probably because he wants to talk, not listen, even if it is her birthday. He has a lot to talk about.

At dinner, Charles steers the last tater tot through a puddle of burger juice and into the remaining smear of green salsa before popping it into his mouth. He wipes his face with an already-destroyed paper napkin and waits for Stephanie to point out the spot he's missed. She's too busy having her mind blown, however.

"You're not just *planning* to help her? You're actually *doing* it?" Stephanie says, her carefully thinned eyebrows arching higher than the squeak in her incredulous voice.

"I'm not entirely sure how far I'm going with it," he says. "For now we're just doing research and considering options. It needs to look natu– "

"You're talking about life and death! It's not just *options*. This woman needs *help*. Like psychiatric help."

This woman is Esther, who almost killed Charles in a freak car accident several months earlier. Where she failed with Charles, she succeeded with three others – a grown woman and two boys – and now she's bedridden and has asked for Charles' help to end her life. The trick is that suicide doesn't pay: as she explained it to Charles, her insurance gives a reduced benefit for suicide. It needs to look natural.

Stephanie says, "It's not like she is dying or has Alzheimer's or something, right?"

"We're all *dying*," Charles answers.

"Spare me the philosophy, Mr. Three Years of Community College!"

"It's true. You or I could be dead before Esther."

"Just because I love you doesn't mean you're not crazy," she answers, and Charles has to laugh. "I want you to promise me to make an appointment for her. She has to have a social worker or something." Stephanie is a counselor at one of the less-ritzy private schools in Baltimore. She thinks her job keeps her thumb on the pulse of the city; Charles thinks it makes her clueless.

"Jesus, Stephanie. She's black, not poor. They don't give you an automatic social worker." He laughs again, differently.

Stephanie's eyes narrow. "From the hospital, asshat. A social worker for her home healthcare. A case manager, a nurse."

"Oh," Charles says. "My bad."

"Someone *trained* to look after her who isn't helping her build a do-it-yourself euthanasia kit."

"She killed three people –" Charles stops himself; he promised he'd keep Esther's secret that despite her claims of amnesia to the police and doctors, she remembers the accident. "She is going to be hauled into court by the families. The parents of those two boys! Doesn't she have the right to end her life?"

"Despair is temporary, but suicide is permanent. How can things ever get better if she ends it?"

"She is bedridden, never to walk again. She is guilt-ridden from mowing down three perfect strangers. She's haunted by her guilt – she can't sleep, she can't read a book, she can't watch movies, and she's stuck in an adjustable bed in her dining room. She can't live with herself. That doesn't sound like despair to me. That sounds like logic."

People cluster around stoops and street corners drinking the warm spring air, screenless windows thrown wide open. Stephanie's words linger in Charles' head, so instead of heading straight home after dinner, he heads to Esther's house. It's late, but she says she doesn't sleep.

He finds himself oddly reassured in her presence. When he's away from her, he doesn't know what the hell he's doing. When he's with her, the mewling complaints in his head disappear; he feels a purpose in life. Figuring out why she killed those people. Exploring the mysteries of the universe. Helping her find a way to end her life that meets her criteria (painless, doesn't inconvenience the neighbors, looks natural). Charles feels permeable around Esther; her goals become his own. Esther has a power over him to make him feel what she feels, and it's more compelling than the rest of his life. It's like being around a baby. The baby cries, you're unhappy. The baby laughs, you join in.

It wasn't until listening to Stephanie at dinner – and he thinks what she said was bullshit – that he realized that when Esther is gone, Charles will have nothing. He will be as aimless as he is during the week when he doesn't see her.

He shuffles up the walk to Esther's house, windows open and lights ablaze, illuminating the spring green bushes and grass in front of her rowhouse. He spots movement in the house and stops; he doesn't want to barge in on her if she has company. He cranes his neck to look inside and confirm there's someone there.

"You looking for somebody?"

A man sits in the shadows on the stoop of the house next door. His tone is not un-friendly, but Charles is out of place here – young white man standing still in the twilight on an old woman's front walk in an all-black neighborhood.

"I was just going to see Esther," Charles says.

"She's home," the guy answers, evenly. He takes a sip from the small bottle – beer? wine? – balanced on his knee. Charles can't see his face well enough in the dark to tell the man's age.

Charles catches another glimpse of movement from inside Esther's house. Esther walks through the doorway to her living room. She moves slowly, hands on doorframe and then sofa for balance, but she's walking.

Walking.

The man on the stoop says, "Are you going to go in? Or … ?"

"I shouldn't have come," Charles says to the man, quickly. "It's too late, and I … I shouldn't bother her."

"She don't get much company," the man says.

Charles starts to respond but then stops: Esther has come now to the window, looking out. Charles wonders for a moment if she sees him, looking outside into the dark from a lit room. But then he sees a flinch, a look of pain flash across her face, and he knows she sees him.

His mind plays back their conversation yesterday: she wants to donate her eyes. A little girl from the neighborhood had a corneal transplant and now sees as good as new. Esther said she'd like to be able to help somebody like that.

She looks out at Charles standing in a pool of light on her walk, her pale green eyes upon his. Esther steadies herself against the window frame, looking silently down at him. Charles turns and leaves without a word. He has many questions, but now he wouldn't believe any of her answers.

Scarecrow

by Lynn Beighley

Seated at the chain restaurant, cameramen in two locations nearby, me and my dad wired for sound. What I know and what I'm guessing:

This is *You Tell Me* reality television show related garbage. (Know.)

I see a couple people from work at a table in the corner. Wow, what a coincidence! (I'm making the most surprised face you've ever seen in your life ever. EVER. Even more surprised than when your mother found out she was pregnant. No, that's not fair. It's a lot more surprised than that.) (Know.)

My dad is still a jerk. He was a jerk when I was a kid, he remains a jerk to this day. (Know.)

Bill will pop out of a giant cake in a few minutes. Naked. (Guess.)

This will not end well. (Know.)

Dad looks at me as though I'm a glass perched on the edge of a table. Clearly, my father the egoist is finally, after twenty-something years, looking out for what's best for his sweet little baby girl.

"Jenn, I," he starts coughing and takes a swig of his scotch. A big swig. A 2-ounce swig. That's not a trivial amount of scotch. And that's on top of what he's already had.

People in reality television land are grinning and probably playing drinking games where they take drinks when he does. I hope they're violently ill and hung over, all of them. Yes.

"Jenn, your young man came by my office today." My young man. "I want you to know that I approve, sweetheart."

Cameras, both of them, are aimed at me. I'm a deer in the laser sights of expert hunters, and my dad has set me up.

I toss back the Manhattan. I say nothing. I smile. Dad says nothing. He looks constipated, in a happy way. I wave at a waiter glancing my way.

All the waiters are glancing my way, everyone in this idiotic fire-roasted-overcooked-steak-free-salty-peanuts-emporium is glancing my way.

This is not me bragging. This is the truth: I'm famous. You know who I am, oh, ninety percent of you. And your friends have already filled you in, oh out-of-the-loop ten percent. They said, "OMG (they say *oh emm gee*), that's the girl Bill Plover's in love with on *You Tell Me*! And there are cameras, holy shit!"

And then I feel a hand on my back. I look up and it's Seamus.

"Jenn, what a surprise," he says, winking. (People who wink, how do they do it? I try, and I always feel like I'm trying to give a secret signal while I'm yelling "LOOK AT ME I'M WINKING LOOK" at the same time.)

I go for suave and polished, not anxious and jittery. I fail, but I stutter out, "Seamus. Seamus. Uh. Dad. Seamus." I flail my right hand about, making straw-filled Scarecrow introductions. (If I only had a brain is apt just now.)

But then I stand up. Enough of the cameras. Enough of my dad, pandering to them. Enough of a white knight swooping in to save me.

E-fucking-nough.

I don't say, "excuse me," like I'm off to the ladies'.

39

(Ordinarily, I would have said, "I have to see a man about a whore," because I think that's hilarious.)

I don't say anything as I grab my bag. I don't look at Seamus, my wannabe hero, or Dad, my wannabe pimp, or the camera people who want to stay in their jobs. I walk out the door.

Just outside, I see Bill Plover in a tuxedo with a bouquet of roses. I stop in front of him.

"Thanks," I say, as I grab the flowers. A thorn bites into my hand.

"Thanks," I say again, as I whop the camera of the bored-looking guy filming it all. Oh, this'll play great in Peoria.

And I sprint to my car, start it, and back out of the lot. My bloody right hand slips on the wheel. My phone is buzzing, and I see Seamus under the awning, looking at me and frowning.

Well, I still have my cat, Pollock.

Let It Be Done

by Andrew Stancek

Zero at the bone. I feel it.

Bed-ridden all those months with Perthes disease, I dreamt even while awake. For hours, I'd lie on the bed, eyes open, seeing not out, but in. Nighttime was best – no distractions, no movement, no sound, no smell, fingers outstretched and mind clear. My breath became regular; my heartbeat slowed; my stomach gurgled and then settled.

All was still.

I wasn't searching, wasn't thinking. I wasn't concentrating, aiming at a resolution.

I emptied.

I feel sorriest for Mom. She had an increasingly hard time with Dad, then suffered through my sickness and Dad skedaddled and now she finds my fame debilitating. She loves me, I know, and doesn't ever say, "Be normal, will you?" just as she wouldn't say it if I had polio, but I know that's what she'd like.

She's a reader. This stillness which for me is a recent gift has always been hers – if such a thing can be transmitted, then I got it from her. In my bedridden times, when I wasn't looking out the window, when I was sleeping or lying there, eyes open, she was still. When she wasn't, she read to me. Hour after hour her voice soothed. She began with the Bible of course, which she reads to herself most of all, and sometimes she didn't have to look down at the page because she already knew that passage, carrying it in her heart.

Mary, do not be afraid, you have won God's favor. Look! You are to conceive in your womb and bear a son, and you must name him Jesus. He will be great and will be called Son of the Most High. The Lord God will give him the throne of his ancestor David; he will rule over the House of Jacob forever and his reign will have no end.

I heard that time and time again, and now I don't need to read it either; it has become a part of me. But Mom suffers no delusion that she's Mary and I'm a Savior. She intoned the consolation of the Psalms and the gore and romance of Exodus and Samuel and Kings; her eyes burned as she recited, "I will show you what is to take place in the future," and rumbled with the twenty-four thrones.

Homer was another whom she read often without eyes on the page. The Trojan Horse was left behind, Laocoön issued his warning and the serpents strangled him. Mom's voice is melodious; she could have been a singer. But she also bellowed. "Beware the Greeks, even ones bearing gifts!"

She recited Longfellow and Millay, Frost and above all Emily Dickinson. So here I am, with zero at the bone, unable to stop for Death, feeling he "kindly stopped for me."

It's been raining for three weeks. I don't expect it to last for forty days, won't dissipate into the crankdom of Doomsday prophecy. I am more conscious of death, particularly my own, since I've been gifted. My life won't be long. Looking out the window at torrents of rain, I see myself dead in it. Stephen Dedalus discovers we are alone and says he will not serve. I am with him on the aloneness and this gift, my many gifts, well, I am not sure I will serve.

Tattarrattat. Palindromes fascinated me even before I was looking at birds. Because of my name I heard "madam I'm Adam" when I was about three and pored through books of palindromes. And now it's all coming together. Zero at the bone and the strangled Laocoön and Joyce's tattarattat and I will not serve.

They're coming. I know they are. I hope Mom will be all right. There's nothing we can do. We both have to say, "Let it be done unto me as you have said."

Barn Party

by Rachel Ambrose

"Sometimes it's not who you know, it's who you don't know," says Blake as he boosts me over a fence to a field waving with soft yellow flowers. "Let's go meet somebody."

His green eyes shine in the bright light, and my stomach does that wonderful swooping thing I've become accustomed to. He's trying to get me over my fear of people, and trying to get me to come out of the house and interact with humanity more often. We've been spending a lot of romantic nights in, so coming out was supposed to be novel.

"Being an artist," he said to me recently, "I've found that creativity can't take place in a vacuum."

Whenever something goes wrong, I just use that as an excuse to stay in. Not that things have gone wrong a lot; Blake is so charming that it's hard for anyone to be annoyed with him.

We're climbing over this fence to get to a barn party one of his artist friends is throwing. I haven't been in a barn since I was at a petting zoo when I was ten years old, so this is going to be interesting. I'm wearing cowgirl boots and a purple cotton dress, and I feel very country. "Let's go *can* something!" I exclaim as we walk across the field hand in hand. My excitement is tempered by my near constant anxiety, so I'm tugging at my dress and fixing my hair without even realizing what I'm doing, and Blake spins me around and kisses me to distract me. We've figured out that this is a near cure-all for the anxiety. This has taken much research and hours of lip locking, and it's been a struggle, let me tell you. An absolute cross to bear.

Crossing the field and entering the barn, I'm surrounded by ladies in dresses and jeans and riding boots, and some of them are even wearing cowboy hats, which might be taking things a little too far, and Blake's air-kissing a lot of them and there are cries of excitement and one of the girls, a pretty brunette with curly hair, even dares to run up and hug him, wrapping her arms around his neck. He laughs and pushes her off, swinging around her to introduce her to me. "Claire, this is Jackie, she's a potter," before high fiving a guy. "Hey, I'm Robin," he says to me, handing me a mason jar filled with pink liquid. "Try our watermelon wine, it's the house speciality." I feel like I've stumbled into some forgotten hippie commune. I take a sip of the drink to steady myself and gasp; it's closer to moonshine than wine, although it's so murderously sweet that it almost tastes good.

Blake never stops touching me during the introductions, and between the alcohol and his hand, I feel almost confident, even though there's a constant buzz of static in my head. Jackie follows us around like a lost, slightly jealous puppy (although that could be my own projection). She makes little comments to him every so often that he sort of nods away, and I feel a little bad. Instead of being freaked out that she's somehow set her sights on Blake, I decide to face things head-on for once, and turn to talk to her.

"So, you're a potter?" I ask her. "I don't really, um, pot. I like those paint-your-own-pottery places, though."

She smiles at me like I'm the most idiotic person in the world. I feel like morphing into a turtle just so I can crawl back into an actual shell and stay there with my glass of moonshine. "I make art with beauty that also serves a purpose within the home environment," she says, and I want to punch her in the mouth because, damnit, I want to be able to say pretentious sentences like that.

"Oh," I say, struggling to come up with a response. "Well, I'm sure your work is important."

"Have you seen Blake's work?" she asks. "It's very chimerical, almost quixotic." She sips her drink, which is a soft green, and doubtlessly more sophisticated than my fruity concoction.

I blink at her. Whose idea was it to pull out the SAT words now? "I have," I say quickly. I actually haven't. Whenever I ask, he tells me he's working on a new series of paintings and that I can see them when they're done. "Have you heard about his new series? He's being very secretive about it."

She smiles knowingly, and I curl my fingers into fists; she better not know him in the Biblical sense, I find myself thinking. "He never reveals his paintings before he considers them complete. He says it interferes with the freedom of his creative brain," Jackie says smugly. As if he has more than one brain. Honestly, this is why I don't hang out with artists very much, and it's a damn miracle I haven't broken up with Blake yet because of it. That might have been the first time that breaking up with him at all has crossed my brain, I realize. It seems important, and I file it away for later introspective analysis. (See, now their vocabulary is seeping into mine!)

I really, really do not care for Jackie. I try to slip away, but she follows me around as I catch back up to Blake, who's making the rounds through the crowd. Luckily, we drink more, and as I have more alcohol, I find more reasons to be amused by Jackie instead of annoyed. She keeps trying to thrust herself into our conversations, but Blake is so focused on me that her attempts are hilarious rather than wrath-inducing. I want to throw out obscure names and concepts like "l'esprit de l'escalier" at her just to see if she knows what they mean. Maybe that's the watermelon wine talking; I'm feeling giddy and spinny and utterly like I could get along with these people given enough alcohol. Then again, alcohol will solve all your problems if you give it enough of a chance, and then it'll kill you as recompense for the gesture.

Miss

by Gill Hoffs

"Can you fit in a quick one before you head for your weekend home?"

Zoe's using her most persuasive honeyed tones, the voice she uses with the trickier clients when their favourite girl's booked out and she wants them to go on a date with another escort instead.

"I'm meant to be getting the train from Deansgate in 2 hours. I only got off a job twenty minutes ago."

"You'll like this one, honest, and it won't take long. Just a gallery opening. No funny business, in and out, canapés and smiles, that's it."

"I'm knackered, babe. Seriously."

"Aw go on. Pleeeeeease?"

I find it hard to turn her down, and she knows it. The opposite isn't true, unfortunately.

I sigh. "Alright."

"You'll do it?"

"Yes, okay. But I'm leaving my stuff at the office and coming there straight after, so you better be waiting, yeah? I'll need a run to Deansgate for a later train."

"That's great, babe, sure. I can do that, no bother. The event runs from three to five, so you shouldn't be *that* late."

She'll take me herself? Bonus!

"What time and who and where? Any special requests?"

48

She gives me the details and I nod, and wonder who let her down and why as I have a quick shower and wash the previous customer's cum from my tits. What to wear? Hmm … Zoe's booked the car for a hasty pickup so I slip on a clingy cotton dress in deepest blue, with just a thong underneath to keep my bush flat, nude heels, and tie my hair in a sleek plait that lies straight and heavy down my back. My planned outfit for home of bootcut jeans, strappy vest, and a sweater, gets tossed in my rucksack with a bra and trainers, and I apply my reddest lipstick (special request) and smoke out my eyes with kohl. A light brush of blusher, not enough to be obvious, and a mint to suck. I'm fastening a heavy bracelet, silver and lapis lazuli, round my wrist when the car arrives. A spray of scent, and I'm done.

The art is obvious and tacky, a tired play on old classics and pop motifs with dogs in bowties playing poker on iPads instead of with cards, and a stuffed squirrel done up like Elvis, and the client is querulous and grey and gropey but the canapés are delicious so I suck it up and smile with shining lips and teeth. I see people assessing us, an unlikely pair, and pat my client's bottom when it looks like I think no-one's looking (though really I can see everything reflected in the cheap not-what-should-be-used-in-galleries glass). One woman nods approvingly and I wonder if she's his friend or just seeing hope for herself at his age.

I try not to clockwatch, and when the client murmurs something about "Perhaps dinner?" his breath warm and wet in my ear, his hand brushing my buttocks, I smile and demur. "So sorry, I'm having a fabulous time but the car's coming at five – prior engagement, you know how it goes. Perhaps next time? Somewhere … intimate?"

He licks his lips and winks at me, and I smile up at him in return.

49

He walks me out to the car, kissing me on the cheek for the benefit of the snoutcasts clustered beside the door, and I touch my fingertips to my lips in a sweet send-off as the driver turns up the volume on what turns out to be some weepy-waily country singer's greatest hits. Her dog's left her for a heavy-drinkin' rodeo-ridin' mime. Or something.

Three songs later, a trio of twangy dirges about the tosspots in the singer's life, and I don't even wait for the car to halt but just open the door as the driver slows beside the office, pop the seatbelt release, and go free.

She's waiting for me with a cup of tea, Earl Grey with milk, and a digestive biscuit. Her hair's pulled back into a messy ponytail, high on the crown of her head like a cheerleader, and I know that means she hasn't been arsed to shower before work, but she looks pretty and girlish and fresh to me.

"How'd it go?"

The blinds are open but we're a couple of floors up and I'm past caring about who sees what, so I slip the straps from my shoulders and drop my dress where I stand, kick off my heels, and take a quick slurp from the cup. Her eyes don't leave my face, so I put the cup on the desk she's sitting on, between the potplant and her thigh, and start getting dressed.

"Fine, fine. Bit boring but the food was okay. Great asparagus tarts."

"They'll make your wee smell."

I pull on my jeans. "Mine only ever smells of roses."

She wrinkles her nose while I hook my bra closed then roll a vest down over my boobs.

"I think I'm the only girl ever who hates them flowers," she says, swinging her legs. "Give me the chocolate Roses over them prickly bastards any day of the week."

Sweater then socks, pause to dunk the biscuit, munch it, stick my feet into my trainers without undoing the laces and wriggle them on against the carpet.

"Don't forget the makeup, babe."

Good point. She beckons me to her and I stand with my thighs touching her knees while she gives me a quick onceover with one of the facial wipes she keeps in the emergency kit on her desk. Wipes, basic makeup, tampons, condoms, lube sachets, mints, and clear nail varnish for stopping runs in stockings before they progress from a hole to a ladder. If anyone's wrecking our girls' underwear, it's our clients.

I can tell from her breath that she's been sucking aniseed balls again, and guess she's managed to keep off the cigarettes for perhaps two days now. She gives up every month and follows a now-predictable routine of willpower, aniseed balls, nicotine gum, nail-biting, boozing, then back on them, with each stage lasting a day to a day and a half. I'm no fan of smoking, but I take her as she is.

"You ready?"

"Pretty much. Look okay to you?"

She winks at me and does that tongue-click thing in the side of her mouth that reminds me of cowboys and dirty cops in movies. I take it as a yes.

In her car, a pink one with plastic eyelashes on the headlights and birdshit on the bonnet, I get to choose the music from her admittedly awful collection. Though tempted by some cheesy pop I know the words to, and something from a pizza advert in the nineties, I decide instead to choose something I've never listened to or played as a backing track for sex.

"You just away the weekend, babe?"

I nod, and she pops another aniseed ball in her mouth from a stash between the seats. I'm not offended at her not offering me one, I'm pleased. She's naturally well-

51

mannered, brought up to be polite, like me, so I can safely assume she's remembered I don't like them. I hope.

"Going to see my aunt, maybe catch up with my brother, too."

"Something special?"

I shake my head. "Nah, just a catchup. If I don't go to them then they start asking to come to me."

"Do they ... ?"

She glances away from the road to raise her eyebrows at me suggestively.

"My aunt does, my brother, no. She's cool with it, I just don't want to be out with family and bump into someone I know."

"I had that once, before I switched to booking and admin. His face was a picture – couldn't work out if my mum was a working girl or a client!"

"God, how cringeworthy."

"I know."

There's a thump and from the sound of it, somebody's been rear-ended up ahead. Zoe taps the brakes and the lines of traffic on our stretch of road grinds to a halt. She crunches the aniseed ball between her teeth, moves her head from side to side then rolls down the window and pokes her head out, straining to see what's going on up ahead.

"Looks like you might miss your train, babe. Smashed it across both lanes, and the drivers are having it out on the tarmac." It's quite warm for May but with the way she's twisting I can't help but notice the little bumps poking through her top. They point up, not down, and I imagine licking them.

She turns her engine off, and looks at me. Smiles, and says, "There's later trains. It'll be fine."

I smile back, I can't help it, and murmur, "It already is."

Saturdays suck, and also Sundays

by Susan Tepper

Pedersen knows he is one of those men earmarked for history. What, or how – the particulars don't interest him nearly as much as the fact that he's been chosen. And not to lay the most benevolent of mankind's gifts onto another. But simply that he was marked from long before his birth. He believes this to be a sacred trust between himself and his maker, wearing it casually like the earflaps with strings that dangle from the sides of his cracked leather cap. He trusts nothing but his own belief system. The one thing not in short supply in Pedersen's life.

Saturdays suck, and also Sundays. The children, his little darlings, tucked away in their backyards, or at some park with parents who watch ready to swoop if a stranger so much as tilts their lips in a semi-smile.

Pedersen cuts some Gouda. Then sits on the floor waiting for Swoon to come out of his rat hole behind the refrigerator molding. He munches the cheese loudly hoping this will attract the white rat.

"You are so fucked!" he cries out when the rat doesn't appear. "I ain't sharing with you."

He takes off the cracked leather cap and flings it across the kitchen. The floor tiles, damaged from years of low-rent

53

families, have dirt stuck in the grooves. From the side of the refrigerator, the rat pokes its quivering pink nose. "So you decided to make an appearance," says Pedersen. "Big of you."

He holds what is left of the Gouda out to the rat.

Sunday, 11th May 2014

Confession

by Jessica McHugh

The service was brighter than the weather. Edward McKenzie's sermon about forgiveness filled the congregation with hope on the dreary Sunday.

Proud to have lifted their spirits, Father Edward retires to the sacristy to decompress. As successful as his sermon had been, his nerves are still on edge. Only a few weeks remain until his teaching position at St. Anthony's begins, and all the preparation in the world hasn't subdued his anxiety.

He drums his fingers on the lid of the Lost and Found jar, his mind drifting. It ventures to canopy beds and ballrooms, places he's afraid to venture in real life. But in fantasy, he delights in gazes falling upon his gowned body in admiration.

The knock on the door jolts him from the reverie. Turning, he smiles as Charlie Kitner's head pokes into the room, a crooked grin creeping up the man's stubbled cheek.

"Sorry to bother you, Father. Are you busy?"

He stands, gesturing for his parishioner to enter. "It's no bother. How may I help you, Mr. Kitner?"

"Charlie."

Edward nods. "How may I help you?"

"I know it's not your usual time, but I was wondering if you would hear my confession."

The parishioner's hands shake on the doorframe. His upper lip collects sweat, and his eyes dart around the room.

Drawing close, Edward says, "My son, you look unwell."

Charlie exhales heavily. "I might be, Father."

He flinches when Edward touches his arm. "Of course I will listen," he replies. "Please, follow me."

But Charlie doesn't follow; he leads. As he strides ahead, Edward can't help but notice the man's athletic physique beneath his suit. His imagination often runs wild when it comes to Mr. Kitner – during sermons, during prayers, even as he stands next to his wife during communion.

Grandma Eleanor's voice fills his mind. *Careful, Edward. This man needs help, not ogling.*

"I understand."

Charlie looks over his shoulder. "Did you say something, Father?"

"Sorry, I was just reminding myself of something," he replies, gesturing to the confessional. "Please, take a seat."

Inside the booth, Edward inhales the distinctive scent of secrets. It's a musty smell, tinged with a floral perfume that recalls memories of his grandmother's closet. As a child, he spent hours there, buried in old clothes to hide from his mother's boozy wrath.

Stirred by comfort and concern, Edward slides open the partition to see Charlie Kitner's face segmented by the rosewood lattice. Although he sits in profile, Edward's focus wanders of its own accord, finding the parishioner's eyes in the smoldering dark. For a few moments, Edward's desire follows his gaze.

"Forgive me, Father, for I have sinned. It's been three years since my last confession."

Holding his hands in his lap, his fingers entwined, Father Edward replies, "What have you to confess, my son?"

"I've had impure thoughts," he replies. "A lot of them. Recently."

"It's human nature, my son. But thoughts are not deeds," Edward says. "Have there been deeds?"

The sounds of fidgeting echo from Charlie's booth. "No," he says. "But these thoughts – they might be unnatural."

"Why do you think that?"

Charlie responds with an audible gulp.

"You're safe here," Edward says. "God is listening, and His forgiveness is immeasurable."

"You said that in your sermon."

"Because I believe it."

"But you don't – you can't –" he huffs, even growls. He sets his face close to the lattice, and Edward clears his throat, scooting to the left side of his seat. "Do you really live the way you want, Father?"

Sweat prickles Edward's forehead. "This isn't about me," he says.

"Yes," Charlie whispers. "Father, I love my wife, but I can't deny that I've had feelings for other people – other *men*."

Edward swallows the rising lump in his throat. "I see."

"Is it wrong? These days it's hard to know the church's position."

"You're married. The church is quite clear on that."

Silence is the great betrayer, and following it with a sigh further robs a lie of its steam. Edward doesn't believe Charlie when he takes too long to say, "I would never cheat on my wife."

"If you're at war, you must do what it takes to find peace."

"That's why I'm here," he says. "I need something to come of this. I'm afraid I won't be able to control myself much longer."

Edward is apt at disguising his desire to help someone in need, but Charlie Kitner is different. He leans too close, speaks too deep. He even peers through the partition to find Father McKenzie's evading eyes.

"Do you believe your desires are wrong?" Edward asks.

Charlie doesn't pause this time. "No. I desire my wife as a man should, but these other desires, these feelings I have when I see a certain man – they feel right, more than any heterosexual relationship I've had. But the Bible says it's a sin."

"The Bible mentions many sins, my son, several of which do not pertain to the modern world."

"So you don't believe it's sinful?"

"I believe ..." Edward's mother threatens to pollute his brain with disparagements, but he blocks her at the first drunken word. "My child, I believe love is love."

"Who do you love, Edward?"

He clears his throat, but his voice is strained when he repeats, "This isn't about me."

Charlie Kitner's fingers hook into the lattice. "Yes, it is. I have feelings for many men, but none so strong as the feelings I have for you."

Edward's lungs empty, and he breaks out in a cold sweat, but he steadies himself by tugging on his crucifix.

"And you seek forgiveness for these feelings," he says.

"No, Father, I seek satisfaction."

Edward shifts in his seat. "Is there anything else you wish to confess?"

"Did you hear me? I said –"

"Yes, I heard you. And so did God. Say five 'Our Fathers', and if you're contrite, you will be forgiven."

Edward has never rushed through a confession before, but he's also never experienced one like this. Flirtation has never been aimed at him, period. Hurrying from the booth, he hears Charlie Kitner's exit, but he doesn't look back. He disappears into the sacristy, locks the door, and snaps open the lid of the Lost and Found jar. The lipstick found by Nelson the altar boy a few months back glistens among the castaways, as if begging for liberation. Reaching inside, he doesn't deny the cosmetic its freedom, or his own.

Hunching over the table, he spins the lipstick out and inhales the distinctive scent. It, too, smells of secrets.

There are no prayers Edward McKenzie can speak to banish Charlie's confession, but with the lipstick pressed to his smile, he can delay guilt for a while.

Giveth and Taketh

by Shane Simmons

"My sister had a miscarriage."

Sandra hasn't mentioned her sister for a while.

"Mum called me in the morning, trying her best to persuade me to go and see Saskia, but I ended up screaming and hanging up the phone." Sitting in the sullen lamplight she pours the cheap red until it almost overflows the rim of her glass. Quickly, she swallows a mouthful before placing the bottle on the coffee table and slides it in my direction. "But then I figured I'd just go, watch karma in action. Maybe tell Saskia it was all her own doing. So I called back and got my mum to pick me up."

"Please tell me you didn't rub your sister's face in it?" I nibble the skin on the joints of my fingers.

"At first Mum did all the talking. I just kept out of the way, watching." She draws a breath so deep it's as if she's sucking all the air from the room. "I didn't expect her to look so bad. I've never seen her like that before. I ended up walking out."

As her eyes redden, I notice the wine in her glass has disappeared before I've even taken my first sip. I carry the bottle over to her, fill her up and leave it at her feet. "I brought plenty, you keep that one."

"Mum came and sat on the doorstep with me. You know, for once she talked some sense. She said she didn't expect me to forgive her. Because I can't, not ever. But all things aside, she will always be my sister. I couldn't punish her, not when she was so …" Her head drops and a tear falls from her cheek. "We went back inside and she left us alone for a bit. Saskia and I ended up crying in each other's arms."

My shoulders droop as I sigh. I'm not sure many people would expect her to have forgiven her sister, but I find myself somewhat proud of her for not taking the cruel route she'd planned.

"Where's Marlon tonight?"

"Night shift. I can't really talk about any of this with him. That's why you're here. You're good with this emotional stuff. And he really doesn't like me talking about my exes."

I don't know where she gets the impression that I'm good with 'emotional stuff'. "We should order some takeaway," I say. "My treat."

Sandra rifles down the side of her chair. A selfish part of me knows that if we don't get something in now, I'll be left to have jam on toast for dinner when I get back to mine.

She tosses me a pile of menus. "You choose, I'm not feeling all that peckish after the day I've had."

I shuffle through them, hoping one will call out to my appetite.

"Anyway," she adds, "there's more."

Of course there's more, it could never have ended there.

"Later, Mum was planning on dropping me home and then going back to stay with Saskia for a bit, but when we walked out of her place I found *him* standing there."

"'*Him*'? Who '*him*'?"

"THAT BASTARD!"

"Oh, Stephen."

She points her finger at me and scowls, "Don't you say his name, not in front of me, not in this flat. Not ever."

I put my hands up to apologise.

"No," she crumples down in her chair, "I'm sorry, it's hardly your fault." She brushes her hair from her face and draws her fingers over her tired eyes. "We walked out, and I spotted him walking up the path. Next thing I remember was that some guy was pulling me off him."

"Pulling you off him?"

"Mum says I booted him so hard in the balls that he keeled over, and that when he was down I just continued kicking the scumbag. When she couldn't stop me, she called some passing guy over to pull me off him."

"Sandra." I shake my head, "Sandra, Sandra." Her name muffles when I drop my face in my hands.

"What? He got much less than he deserved. If I'd've known he was going to turn up I would have been ready to give him a kitchen knife vasectomy."

Under normal circumstances I'd laugh right about now, but I don't. Sandra's brow is furrowed, her fists rolled up into tight balls, jaw clenched shut.

I return carrying some warm boxes and a couple of plates from her kitchen. Placing it all on the coffee table I start sharing out the pizza, garlic wedges and chicken wings. "I'm making you a plate, otherwise tomorrow you're going to regret downing all that wine on an empty stomach." I get a huff in response. "So, what happened after you were removed from St– ... that bastard?"

"Mum dragged me back indoors. Can you believe Saskia wanted to see him? I thought she must've been crazy, so I slapped her to wake her up. You know, like they do in the movies."

I pause as I spoon sour cream dip on the side of her dish, mid-dollop.

"And I'm going to assume that didn't help the situation at all?"

She shakes her head from side to side. "Mum let that bastard in, sat him in the kitchen, and then sent me on my way." Her arms flail through the air before landing back on the arms of her chair with a thump. "And to top it off I had to get the bus home."

I hand the plate to her and sit back down. It's not long before she's wrestling with webs of stringy cheese between her teeth.

"Are all families like this?" We both pause and peer at each other. "Hmm, I guess you've got an idea what I mean, what with your ... you know, mum and dad. And your sister. You have got a sister, haven't you? You never really talk about her."

I pick up her remote control and turn the television on.

"It's complicated. So for the rest of tonight I prescribe us some crap TV, more pizza and no more family-induced traumas."

Poised to bite into the chicken wing in her hand, she shrugs her shoulders, "Fair do's. You've had to suffer enough of my dramas that it's only fair you burden me with some of yours, one day."

She doesn't know that I don't mind. I'd rather she was the one pouring her heart out. Talking only reopens old wounds. And I prefer keeping them shut.

Cosy

by Michelle Elvy

"So, are you ready for your exams, Stephen?"

"Yes."

"And graduation?"

"Yes."

"And college?"

"Yes."

"Do you have anxieties about leaving home?"

Fuck. This was going to go on forever. Stevie had agreed to *see someone* for his parents. He felt bad that they worried so much about him, and he felt even worse that he didn't talk to them much these days. He wanted his parents to stop worrying, so he'd agreed to come sit in this expensive leather chair (*pretty comfy, come to think of it, but who has yellow chairs? Is that really so healthy for all the crazy depressed people who must come sit here an hour at a time? Really? Sunny yellow chair for your dark mood to sink right into?*) for an hour because he thought it'd be a quick way to reassure them that everything was fine. *Anxieties?* Sure. Of course. What the fuck.

"Do you want to talk about the accident?"

"No."

"Why not?"

"Lucky's dead. Nothing else to say."

"And you were close to Lucky."

He'd seen scenes like this in the movies – the Concerned Adult asking the Troubled Teen about his feelings. The teen shifting uncomfortably in his comfy leather chair – but in the movies those chairs are not sunny yellow. And now all he can think is *Christ, I'm in one of those movies, with a ridiculously concerned adult and a ridiculously happy chair.*

"What's so funny?"

Stevie hadn't realized he was smiling. He was thinking about all the movies he'd seen with scenes like this, and how stupid it always looked, the Troubled Teen with nothing to say, the Concerned Adult with so much experience asking all the right questions, gently, gently. Did he have anxieties? Hell, yeah. But they had nothing to do with college. They had more to do with the fact that he'd been thinking about *not* going to college – not yet anyway. He'd been dreaming more and more about his Great Grandpa Gus and an old sailing boat, and he felt the vague notion that he'd like to go exploring. Which of course he'd not admitted to anyone. *Go exploring.* What the fuck. What did that even mean? He figured college could wait, that for a kid like him with decent enough grades college would still be there next year, or the year after. He didn't feel the urge to rush off to the drunken embrace of other freshmen to "grow". That's what adults were always saying: *you grow so much at college.* He had a cousin who got kicked out of college for getting drunk and tearing up the landscaping of the president's house and shitting on his lawn. No thanks, he was not quite ready for that kind of experience yet. He hadn't broken into a car since Lucky died and he wasn't into institutionalized adventure. He needed to be alone. He needed to get away from here, from his loving parents, from Concerned Adults. And from Lucky's ghost.

Lucky. Christ, how'd he have to die? Five people in the car and it was Lucky who died. Front passenger's seat, no seatbelt, feet on the dash, reefer between the lips, then windshield impact and oblivion in the span of a nanosecond. Lucky's last micro-moment. Stevie has played this over and over in his head, tried to live in that moment. He crawls back there to stay, scratches his way in with Lucky, but it's always fleeting. He feels the car lurch and bend, he senses wheels locking, hears a faint gasp from Manny at the wheel, and then he stops his mind to focus on Lucky from his backseat position – he's behind Manny so he has a good view. The car is bending around and starting to flip, flying in the air at great speed and height. He sees Lucky's hair waving around in an unnatural way. He sees Lucky turn to Manny and grin his big stupid grin and start to say something but then he can't hear anything, because suddenly the car lurches another time and Stevie is airborne. He tries to climb back through the window and into the car with Lucky in those next few moments, but he knows that the real reason he can't do it is because there are no more moments for Lucky. Time has stopped. Head and windshield shatter in a million little pieces, cracked together in one last moment, tiny bits of glass and tiny bits of skull a mingling mosaic. Stevie wills one more moment in for Lucky, because one more moment could make a difference. But time stops and Lucky has no more moments. And Stevie is airborne and stretching across the sky in a spatial-temporal dreamscape, leaving his friends behind – leaving Lucky – and soaring toward a faraway seascape where waves rise up like mountains and ships toss like toy boats. In the moment Lucky becomes one with the windshield Stevie is escaping to the Southern Ocean where he rendezvous with his Great Grandpa Gus on the dark hulk of a great oak ship, tumbling in the wintry grey morning sky above a southern Maryland cornfield while the whaler floats up toward him.

"Stephen? Do you want to say anything about the accident?"

"No."

"Do you want to tell me about the dreams?"

The dreams are always the same. Stevie is lifted on a blanket of warmth, surrounded by a frozen January sky. It's May now but he's still stuck in January in his dreams, cushioned on cotton candy clouds above the Maryland cornfield with Great Grandpa Gus rioting along on an old oak schooner in heavy seas below. The ship is breaking up, the canvas, the rigging, the hull, and Stevie reaches for it, then for Gus, and now for Lucky but his fingers slip through all of it – canvas-wire-oak-flesh – and he twirls away in the tornado-black air. Panic now rises in his gut because his voice won't reach from southern Anne Arundel County to Cape Horn where a great sailing ship is tearing apart at the seams nearly a century before. And it won't reach Lucky either.

The dreams occur often, and they are real. They are horrifying and exhilarating. But he can't explain that. He can't play the role of Troubled Teen spilling his guts to the Concerned Adult. Not here, not in this ridiculously comfy chair.

"Stephen, do you want to tell me about the dreams?"

"No. The dreams aren't real."

Two hours later Stevie is walking in the open air and breathing easy. He hears a voice and it's dream-reality again, because this is a voice he thinks about all the time, sleeping and waking, a voice he can't escape. A birdsong in the breeze. But he knows, even though they've become closer in the last couple months, that he can't ever be with Ellie Smithers. Lucky's girl.

"Hey! Hey, you, wait up!" She jogs up behind him, and takes his arm. "Where you going?"

"Down to the pier."

"Can I come?"

"'Course."

"So ... how was it?" He is startled by Ellie's directness, because this feels like a secret he should keep, one of his many. He doesn't want to burden Ellie with his anxieties, how he sees Lucky in the moment of impact, head on windshield, and how that moment seems to coincide with his moment of flying through the window and escaping; how he thinks he may skip college for now and do something else instead and how that idea scares the crap out of him; how he sees his Great Grandpa Gus all the time now, not only in his dreams but even in waking moments – by the old pier, at the post office, in the back garden by the crape myrtle. He has wondered if he's going nuts, but he feels deep down that this is all just part of his reality, and he has a vague notion that it'll be alright if he can just get out of here. But he can't get away if he's walking down the street with Lucky's girl.

A queasiness overcomes him and he's about to think up an excuse to turn and go the other way, away from Ellie and the heat of her body which he can feel next to him through his light windbreaker and jeans, all the way down to his socks, when she says, "You know, I've been meaning to tell you you're a star in our house. I mean, with Sylvie. She talks about you all the time ever since you helped her bury her bird."

"That was a long time ago now."

"I know, but it meant a lot to her. She loved that bird."

"Yellow Bird."

"Yeah. Yellow Bird."

Ellie lets out a little high-pitched chuckle and it reminds him of that day back in March, how quiet it was sitting in the back yard and helping Ellie's little sister bury her canary, and how they sang together and held hands, and how Sylvie looked so *peaceful*. And how Ellie – whose voice he loved and dreamed about both sleeping and waking – could not carry a tune.

He laughs.

"What?"

"Nothing."

"Come on, tell me. What?"

"You know you can't sing, right?"

Ellie laughs too. "Yeah, I know. But I sing for Sylvie. She likes it."

"Are you kidding? She *loves* it."

Then Ellie takes Stevie's hand and squeezes it and says, "Stevie? Tell me about your dreams?" and he finds himself saying out loud, for the first time ever, "The dreams are real."

The Luckiest Sonofabitch on Earth

by Len Kuntz

Outside of Omaha, I stop at a bar and count how many women I've slept with since finding out about my wife's affair. I get to ten and a half, the half being a prostitute who was actually a very convincing cross-dresser.

I think about the life I've left behind, the house on the lake, a home that always felt more like a prison or mausoleum. I try to tell myself things could be worse, they can always be worse. After all, it's a grand adventure I'm on, traveling across the country without any idea where I'm heading, an unorthodox journey that just might be the bravest thing I've ever done.

I drain my glass, relishing the burn, and order another scotch. Even though we're halfway through a sunny May, it's dark in the bar, quiet too, except for a garbled juke box that plays antique Buck Owens and The Buckeroos.

The guy on my right keeps farting into his barstool while reading a tattoo magazine and the guy on my left is busy flexing and unflexing his prosthetic hand. I try not to stare or make eye contact, but I can't look away, and after a moment he says, "I'm still getting used to this thing," adding that his name is Gary.

Gary lost his limb in Kandahar when he was on patrol, saw a ten-dollar bill sticking out from a clump of dirt in the road, and an IED exploded after he reached for it. Gary chuckles. "Moral of the story – greed'll get you every time." He says he's the luckiest sonofabitch on earth, says he could have easily had his head blown off, or any number of body parts.

Hearing this should make me feel grateful for my life, but I'm still wallowing in self-pity and all that optimistic bullshit I'd been contemplating moments ago now feels like tripe.

Gary asks me if I'm married. Gary asks me where I'm from, asks me all kinds of questions before wondering if I'd like to go get high.

Outside, back behind the bar, there are half a dozen garbage cans overloaded with beer and liquor bottles. It smells briny.

Before lighting up, I think of Lana and her boyfriend – the pair I'd met by chance at a convenience store – and what we'd smoked, so I say, "This isn't laced with anything, is it?"

Gary looks at me like I've just told him his kids are ugly.

I take a long drag and hold it until I'm about to implode. Gary smiles a big shit-eating, I-lived-through-hell-and-I'm-still-alive grin, and I think I really like Gary and maybe I should use his example to reset my own pessimism.

Since we're doobie brothers now, I take a good look at Gary's hand. The prosthetic is a strange one, like a robot's, only with plastic where the metal should be, and see-through screws. He catches me looking and says, "It's the latest model."

"It's fancy."

Eddy takes a long hit and tamps the lit end of the joint against his plastic hand where it leaves a gray smudge similar to a spider that's been crushed.

With his other hand, he pulls a pistol out of his jacket and says, "Get on your knees, Fuckhead."

I'm thinking I'm stoned already and that this is a hallucination, but then Gary swipes the air, his claw scraping a good section of my face.

"What the hell?"

"I've shot better than you, and I'm not the patient type."

I get on the ground. It's covered with broken glass and sharp rocks. My knees sting. I notice Gary's wearing steel-tipped cowboy boots.

"Hand over your wallet, then put your hands on the ground, ass up, doggy-style."

I don't know whether to be more frightened about being robbed or the possibility of being buttfucked by some brute with a hook for a hand.

He stuffs my cash into his pocket and tosses the wallet so that it slaps my face and a creased photo of my wife flips out.

"You never asked where I'm from," Gary says. "You never asked a damn thing about me."

He's right, I hadn't.

"You're a selfish prick."

He's probably correct about that as well.

"Now get face down on the ground and don't get up until you've counted to five hundred."

"Hey, how about –"

In one swift move, Gary rams his boot tip, hitting the bulls-eye between my buttocks.

"I told you I was impatient," Gary says, spitting before walking away.

My anus is enflamed. It's hard to concentrate. I count to forty-five and stagger to my feet. I go back in the bar and ask about Gary, but they say they don't know any Gary.

"Captain Hook," I say, making my hand a claw. "The bruiser that was sitting on the stool right there, next to me."

The bartender and fart guy look at me like I'm an idiot.

I start to get angry and ask again.

"You cause a fuss," the bartender says, "I'll call the sheriff."

"I'm just asking about Gary."

"And we just told you we don't know any Gary."

I figure they're probably all in cahoots, but what can I do. "Fine, then give me another scotch."

"No way, Jose."

"Why not?"

"We have the right to refuse service to whoever we want."

"This is fucked."

"Watch your pie hole."

I go over to an ATM that sits by a video poker machine featuring Kim Kardashian's enormous ass and cleavage. I withdraw a hundred, then take out the maximum it will allow in a day, leaving the bar with my middle finger upraised, my own ass smoldering, while I wonder how much a gun costs.

Fifth Inning

by Michael Webb

I never hurry when I know the kids are at the game. Our opponents are headed out of town after the game, so an early start, the 'businessperson's special', eases their travel woes and, as long as we don't fall into one of those 11-9 fracases, gives us a rare afternoon at home. I am anxious to see them, but I know there are bathroom trips and ice creams to eat and goodbyes to say, so I take my own time showering and dressing.

There is a light mood in the locker room, anticipating the leisure to come, along with the game result, a crisp 3-2 win that we finished in a quick 2 hours and 10 minutes. I contributed, ending a seventh inning jam on one pitch and then only needing 10 more to negotiate the 8th, before handing the game to Tex to lock it down. I dress quietly, then make my way down the hallway towards the player parking lot.

The lot is gently managed chaos, with more SUVs than usual bucking for position to exit the garage. I look down the line of cars, and four cars back is my own Yukon, black and foreboding with a distinctive scratch on the driver's side mirror. I stroll down to it. The car I am next to, a boxy BMW, rolls its window down. I see the hawk-nosed face of our starting shortstop, Juan Nogales, looking at me from the passenger seat. A round-faced woman, her tiny arms and legs straining to reach the controls around an enormous belly, is driving, scowling at him, and then at me. He looks at me angrily, his brow knitted with tension.

"Twainie?" he says.

"What's up?" I reply.

"Settle something for me," he says. "Lucasita doesn't believe me about last night."

I think about last night's game, a 9-7 loss, in which Juan had saved my bacon with a diving stop that would have charged me with two runs if he had not snagged it. I thought I knew what he meant.

"The dinner?" I venture.

"Yes! You took me out for dinner because I saved your ass. Again," he says, smiling.

"Sure did. Why? Was he home late?" I say, looking into her enormous brown eyes. She appears deep into what my wife calls the "Fuck You" stage of pregnancy, when all the magic and wonder of it has drained away, and it's purely an endurance trial, trying to get to the end before killing anyone. The seatbelt is forced aside by her huge, taut belly, which looks entirely too large for her tiny frame.

"3 am," she says in a softly-accented voice.

I sneak a glance at Juan, and our eyes lock. Just like when we pick a runner off second, I know his intentions, and I follow his lead. "I'm so sorry," I say earnestly to her. "I didn't mean to keep him out that late. I promise, I'll make sure he gets to bed on time from now on. He's going to need his sleep," I continue, gesturing at her stomach.

"Yes," she says shyly, curling one hand underneath the impossible weight of it. "He will."

"See?" he says as she rolls the opaque window back into place. I make my way down the row of cars, sliding around and into the front seat of my own car. I silently weigh the lie I just told against the truth that Nogales probably saves me two dozen runs a year with acrobatic plays.

"What was that?" my wife says.

"Just guy talk," I say to her. "Juan's wife is about to pop, isn't she?"

"Yup," she says, the car creeping forward. "She's miserable, though. Poor thing. She says he tried to say you took him out to dinner after the game last night! Imagine!" she continues, shaking her head.

"That's ridiculous," I say, staring at the brake lights in front of us.

"I want pizza for dinner, Dad," I hear from the back seat.

"As long as it's OK with Mom, sport. You got it," I say.

Cross Purposes

by James Claffey

In the shade of the rowan tree he sits down, fallen branches crunching under his weight. Loneliness. The death of his parents seems unnatural. Since his mother's visit he's not slept well at all in full sight of the wardrobe from where she'd appeared. Stones unturned, the Bird's hands search the rough mud-caked surfaces for comfort. The smoothness of time, the brazen feel of the rocks, gives him some measure of solace. Only this morning he'd prayed for the French woman to return from her travels so he could allow a mite of hope to penetrate his sour mood.

May, and the trees in bloom, pink and red blossoms all along the river, a time of renewal, energy returned, even, though he'd never admit it to anyone, the hope of love's rekindling. Stupid, it was, too. How he could possibly hold her interest, with his talk of flies and rods, of wild plants and tortured animals.

The Bird turns over and over the few kind words Melodie said to him. Her accent, the delicate fingers, her smile. Then he remembers his mother's jewelry box, the musical one with the tiny dancer turning pirouettes to sprung music. Sadness freefalls, the weight of his grief rooting him to the spot under the tree. Several thrushes sing in the branches, sweet songs, natural sound, no wound springs there, he thinks. A drop of rain plops on the end of his nose, hard. He remains rooted. There's no escaping a drenching, he knows. The water will cleanse him, bring his sadness to a new place, let him release the cry stuck in his throat these many months.

As a boy the Bird couldn't stop searching the trees around the town for eggs. Speckled blue his favorites. The day his father caught him in the shed with a handful was the first real whipping he'd ever received. Even now, the birdsong so beautiful, the sting of his father's hand is fresh on his cold skin. Then, a boy, his skin pitted with acne scars, he sought love every bit as much as today. All through his teenage years failure stalked him like a stray pup, tailing at his heels to the door of his house.

His thoughts are brought back to the moment by a loud "Halloo!" from the road a bit away towards the town. "Bird! By God, that's a bitter day that's in it," calls out Georgie Pepper, the postman, astride the black Raleigh with the wicker basket in front, the cavernous postbag swung over his shoulder like a dead creature.

"'Tis, for certain. There'll be frost on the pisser tonight and no mistake," he says in return. The postman raises a hand from the handlebars, wobbles in a desperate manner, and pushes on into the wind.

The beautiful sky, the thick clouds separating into strewn cotton balls, lifts the Bird's spirits somewhat, and he decides he might as well go back to the house and have a bath with a nice drop of brandy in the water to keep the chills at bay. He'd seen his mother pour the Hennessey into her tub for as long as he could remember, and it strikes him as a better way to close out the day than sitting on damp earth and waiting to catch his death of cold.

As he stiff-legs the pedals of the Raleigh to get up the hill in front of the town, the Bird spots a collarless Alsatian dog rooting about the verge by a telephone booth. "Here, boy! Here, boy," the Bird calls, slowing to a stop. He swings his leg over the crossbar, pushes the bike slowly, and clicks his fingers and the dog shakes a head and lets a long pink tongue droop from its mouth. Slow, step, slow, step, the Bird approaches and the dog lowers its head and lets the Bird scratch behind its ears. "Good boy, there's a good boy." The rain pelts and the Bird opens the phone booth door and slips inside. The Alsatian nudges its snout in the door and pushes its way in. Before the Bird can push back and keep the dog at bay, it's inside and has both front paws on the Bird's shoulders. Some humanity stares back at the Bird as he turns his face to avoid the licking pink of the tongue.

Murphy, the plasterer, drives past the phone box and seeing the Bird's bicycle, slows and honks three times. From inside, the Bird sees the car drive by and tries to slide past the giant beast pinning him in by his shoulders. "Arrah, good boy! Let me past," he says. The dog licks again and the Bird feels a curious sensation in his gut, and a spasm of heat washes over him, and for a moment, his mind wandering away to dark and dangerous places. Before he can gather his thoughts, a rap on the glass startles him, and the priest cocks his head and raises an eyebrow in greeting.

By the time the Bird pushes the dog away and steps out into the rainy day once more, the road is deserted and his bicycle is on its side at the grass verge. "Go on, now. Go home," he tells the dog. The creature sits placidly by the phone booth, a questioning stare in its eyes. Back on the bike again, the Bird pushes off into the rain and leaves the dog pawing at the door of the booth, eager to return to the relative warmth and dryness it offers.

Inside McKettrick's, the crowd is thick and the air is filled with cigarette smoke. He pushes his way to the counter and orders a whiskey to settle his nerves. God, but that dog was a powerful beast, he thinks. Across from him on the far side of the counter, Murphy is supping his pint. He catches the Bird's eye and lets out a tremendous howl. Three or four of his pals, drinkers of renown, follow suit. In moments the entire bar is filled with howling, Murphy scarlet in the face, the tears rolling down his face. "You bloody dog fucker, you!" Murphy yells at the Bird. "Pervert!"

The Bird reddens, turns to old McGettrick and begins to explain about the dog and the phone booth and the rain, but he can't be heard over the howls of the drinkers. He fishes in the pocket of his trousers for a few quid and leaves the money on the counter, fleeing for the safety of the street, forgetting completely to ask for his drink.

Saturday, 17ᵗʰ May 2014

The Worst Thing

by Gwendolyn Joyce Mintz

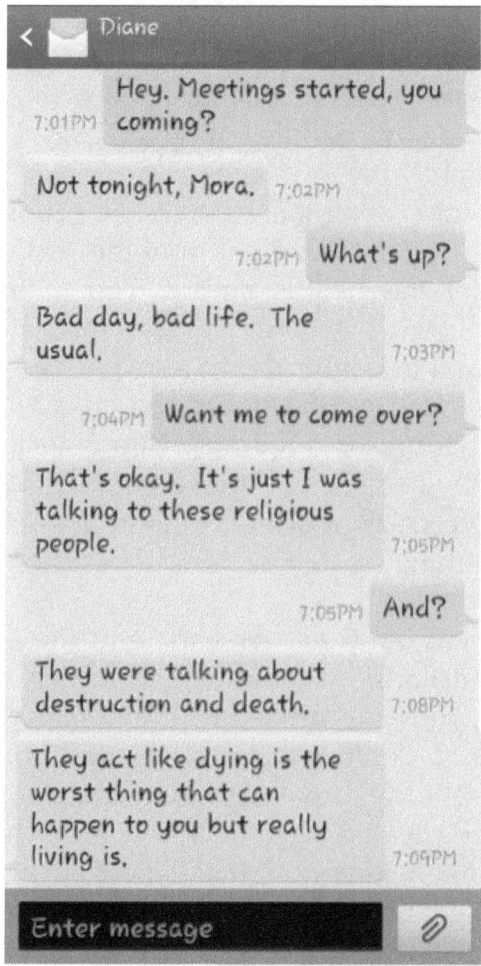

Grace

by Stephen V. Ramey

A river rolls into a vast black sea. There is no churn, no rippling struggle, just the unceasing flow of water, warm into cold. I feel a bubble of grief, and I wake, teeth clenched so tightly my jaws ache.

Mystery, our long-haired cat, is curled atop the comforter in a shard of sunlight from the bedroom window. Anne's side of the bed is empty. The radio-clock reads 10:19.

Sunday used to be our day to sleep in. For the past year, Anne has attended a Spiritualist church a few miles from New Castle. She met the founder, Kim Fogely, at a potluck lunch, and they became fast friends. Kim is supposed to be a medium. I've never met her, but Anne seems convinced there is something to it. Her atheism is more fragile than mine.

I pet the cat between her ears, and those golden eyes open. She leans into my hand, content within the warmth of her sunshine. Her chin sinks down. She licks the matted fur on her chest. I don't remember the last time she really groomed herself. My throat chokes up. At eighteen, Mystery does not have much longer in this world. This, of course, reminds me that neither do I, most likely.

"I should get up." I lift the covers and gently roll away, then fluff a blanket against the cat's spine. She nestles in.

Her front claws knead in and out. "I should work on the book," I say, but I balk at the thought of sitting at that desk, staring at that screen. Five months and I'm still stuck on Chapter Two.

In Chapter One, a mysterious man enters a small town hardware store. The clerk is drawn to his certainty; the store owner notes there's no car in the lot or on the street out front. How did he get here? In Chapter Two, we learn the man, named Zechariah for now, has come from the future to warn against our self-destructive behavior: unfettered reproduction, ecological desecration.

These issues interest me, but no matter what I try, the dialogue will not ring true, the characters will not step off the page. I've cut and pasted and re-cut and re-pasted paragraphs so many times the whole thing is a blur in my mind, and the online thesaurus is exhausted with my constant queries.

I look out the window. Blue sky, not a cloud. Below our house, church spires rise from the bowl of the city. Saint Mary's bells will ring at eleven. Usually I stay in bed until I hear them. Today I am too restless.

This book is supposed to be my masterwork – that's what I keep telling Anne – but the truth is it's just the usual science fiction cautionary tale. You could fill a shelf with versions of this idea. I have nothing original to say. Why do I keep trying? I recall the feeling of grief from my dream, and it swells inside me to the verge of bursting.

I pull off my pajamas and hurry into my best black jeans and white button-down shirt. *I have to get out of this house.*

Downstairs, I leave a mound of food on Mystery's plate before stepping into the crisp morning air. Trees are budding along the back edge of our property. A cardinal sings. The world is emerging from its depression.

I stride down the hill, down the street, black leather shoes scraping through Saint Mary's asphalt lot into the city's heart. Cars blur, a traffic light turns. I come to another church built from red brick and surrounded by a wrought iron fence. I remember reading that it was purchased by a new denomination.

Stained glass windows are inset high on the wall facing me, a Haloed-Jesus-With-Sheep flanked by broad green leaves curled into horns of plenty. Second thoughts percolate as I step into the building's shadow. I haven't been to church in forty years. I remember the homeless woman at Tent City – was her name really Tomorrow? – saying the river called me. There's no river here, just a building, a stretched black shadow.

We are our own master. And yet I'm here when I could be reworking Chapter Two, or rewriting Chapter One, or outlining the way forward, or even petting Mystery to a steady purr.

I barely pull the wrought iron handle, and the door swings open. The entryway is well lit: white walls, polished granite floor. An alcove holds tapered candles in pewter stands beneath an oil painting of Jesus bleeding from his crown of thorns. Ahead, stairs lead up and down. For a moment I don't know which way to go, but of course up is the answer. The downward path probably leads to a basement, a kitchen, a catacomb.

I climb to a landing twice as wide as the stairs. Double-doors stand closed before me. I'm surprised by how quiet it is. Maybe the congregation is praying.

I crack open a door, planning to slink through and into the nearest pew before anyone notices. Rank upon rank of empty pews greet me, the auditorium funneling down to an altar bearing a dais and two pedestals holding vases of yellow and white flowers. Jesus hangs on the wall, arms outstretched upon the cross. His eyes are downcast. Dull. Bored.

"Welcome!" A woman appears from a corridor near the altar. She's wearing a flowered dress, her graying hair is pinned up into a bun, and I can see her vivid red lipstick from here. "Have you come to pray?" She strides up the carpeted aisle. "We hold services on Saturday and Wednesday evening."

I let the door close behind me. "Isn't this a church? I thought Sunday –"

"God is everywhere and everywhen," she says. "He doesn't care when we pray, only *that* we pray." She extends her hand. "My name is Grace. My husband and I are pastors here. And you are … ?"

"Stephen." I clasp her hand. Her fingers are boney. "I was out for a stroll. I've always wanted to see the inside of this building."

"And you chose today?" Grace's eyebrow lifts. "Are you sure there's nothing more important going on? God knows, and He will tell me if you do not."

"I don't believe in God."

"He believes in you."

"Then why did He give me cancer?"

According to Anne, who has a background in biology, cancer cells are just normal cells gone wild. They don't know how to stop growing or when to die. By one estimate, the sum total of cells cultured from Henrietta Lacks' cancer in 1951 would weigh more than 50 metric tons now. Surely that is one version of God.

Grace licks her lips. "I doubt very much that God gave you cancer. More likely you brought that upon yourself, or it might be a simple accident of fate."

"Then I'm wasting my time here."

Grace's arms spread wide. "No, Stephen. Accept Jesus into your heart and –"

"God will cure me?" I push my fists into my pockets.

"Perhaps," Grace says with a shrug. She clasps her hands between us. "Perhaps not. It's not our place to demand a price for faith."

"Then why bother?" I say.

"Because it is the way to heaven." Grace's mouth pushes into a pitying frown. "God judges us not on our rhetoric, but by our actions." Her eyes glisten. "Tell me, Stephen, do you do nothing out of simple kindness?"

"Of course," I say. I think of tucking the blanket around Mystery, filling her plate before I left. "I pick up trash when I walk."

Grace nods. "You see? The impulse is there. We just need to help you focus it."

This is crap. Yet, I don't want to leave. Sunlight slants from stained-glass-Jesus, illuminating the brighter colors and mystifying the dark. Dust motes dart through the beams, riding unseen currents. The chapel is chilly with drafts.

Grace leads me to the altar. She kneels. "Pray with me, Stephen."

"I can't." I stand a stride behind her, shoulders curled forward like a vulture. "I don't know how."

"Of course you do," Grace says. "Our Father, who art in heaven ..."

"I can't do this." I edge away. My legs hit something, and I stumble unceremoniously back onto a padded bench. Books stare at me from the pew ahead. *Holy Bible. Hymns.* The Bible is black, the hymn book's cover maroon.

Grace looks over her shoulder. "Do not fear His presence, Stephen. Go with it. You must think of life as a stream."

Of course! I think. That's what I've been missing. That's what the Tent City woman was trying to tell me. My eyes find the Bible, and sensation lifts through me like gravity reversing. *You must think of life as a stream.* This is the missing element in my novel. The character hasn't come back to warn us, but to change our religion. A God of the future, not the past. *Our Father of the Future, the god who awaits.* I glance at Grace. She's still talking, but her voice is only a distant hum. I don't even notice I am standing until her eyes follow me up.

"I have to go," I say. "I have to write. I haven't felt this passionate in a year."

Grace's head tilts. Her eyes evaluate. I can almost hear her thinking, *Has God embraced this man, or Satan?*

I step into the carpeted aisle. "Thanks," I say. "Thanks so much, Grace. You've helped me more than you can know." I turn and walk away, faster, until my feet can barely keep up. Up the aisle, down the steps, out the door, through the wrought iron gate, and onward until Jesus in the window is but a smear of color in a red brick wall.

A Passing

by Gay Degani

Outside in the brisk May air, warming her hands on her coffee mug, her silk kimono wrapped tightly around her, Sybil waits for Mars German and his crew to show up. The tree guys came yesterday: turned the fallen oak into firewood, ground out the stump. Makes her sad to think nothing is left of that grand old tree but a lumpy hole in the ground. It's been four months since the windstorm blew through the area and knocked over 600 trees, the oak falling on one of Sybil's rental houses.

She looks up just as a shiny Lexus pulls to the curb. A large man, maybe late fifties or so, wearing a work shirt and fashionably-ripped jeans, climbs out of the car and strides toward her. Then she recognizes him. Louisa Renke's son, and she knows right away why he's here.

"Mr. Renke," she says as he approaches. "Not bad news, I hope."

His eyes shift beyond the wrecked little house at the front of the property to where his mother lived in the bungalow at the back. He works his jaw, swallows, and says, "She died yesterday. It was okay. In her sleep. She was ready."

"I'm so, so sorry." Sybil puts her hand on his forearm and squeezes. A muffled sob erupts from the big man. Everyone, no matter who they are, she thinks, comes to a moment when something reaches into their gut and wrings out such a sound. "Can I help you with anything?" she asks.

He doesn't answer; she's patient. She doesn't let go of his arm. Then he places his hand on hers, and asks, "Will you help me to find something for her to wear?"

His words conjure up a casket, rosewood maybe, satin trim – Ray has money – with Louisa's face softened in death, carefully applied make-up mocking her with blush. "Of course," she says.

"I'll keep paying rent until I get all her affairs in order," he says as he slips his key into the lock of Louisa Renke's front door. "Through next month at least. Is that enough time for you to find another tenant?"

"That'll work out fine." Jamie comes unbidden to Sybil's mind. If the girl comes back, even though she's been away four months, she and the kids will need a place to stay. She'll keep it empty for a while. And no need to rebuild the front bungalow. Clear the space instead, she thinks. Plant grass, roses. Build an arbor.

Inside the house, the musty smell reminds Sybil of how long it's been since Ray Renke put his mother into assisted living, yet the place has remained exactly the same, the crocheted throw over the arm of the sofa, the stack of crossword puzzles on the coffee table next to the remote. She hasn't thought of Louisa at all these last few months. The old woman had been moved before Christmas, had missed the big storm, and for this, Sybil was grateful. The thunderous sound of the oak falling on Jamie's bungalow would have given Louisa a heart attack.

From the closet, Ray pulls out a stiff, old-fashioned pantsuit with manly shoulder pads, an outfit Sybil had never seen the old woman wear.

"This is how I remember her," he says. "In this suit, or one like it, kissing me on the forehead as she dashed out the door for work. I remember the back of it better than the front."

"I can't remember. What did she do for a living?"

"Advertising, downtown at Bradshaw's Department store. She rode those copy-writers like a trail boss. Whipped 'em. That's what she used to say. I guess no one would get that today."

"I get it. I used to watch *Rawhide*," Sybil says.

Ray smiles at this. "Me too. She was a pistol. Women didn't do that back then, work a man's job when other women were hanging laundry on clotheslines."

"I hung laundry on clotheslines," says Sybil, and for a moment she remembers herself shaking out damp clothes, pegging them to a rope strung between the back of her house in Nebraska and a lone hackberry tree. "But I wanted to be like your mother."

"I guess she'd choose this suit to be buried in," says Ray.

"Anything in there you'd prefer?"

Ray looks up, as if this thought would never have occurred to him. "I don't think –" He turns back to the closet.

A car door slams outside and Sybil tiptoes into the living room to peek out the front door. Mars German, son of the old man who lives in the other front bungalow, strides toward Jamie's ruined house while $8-an-hour laborers jump off the back of a rusty pick-up truck. Mars has turned out to be a handy man to have around. Well, he knows what to do, she thinks, he doesn't need me to supervise, and leaving the door ajar to let in fresh air, she returns to the bedroom.

Ray stands in the middle of the floor holding a summer print dress with yellow, red, and aqua bouquets scattered across a white background, scooped neck, cap sleeves, a red belt cinching the waist, and a full pleated skirt. His face is shining.

"Oh!" Sybil gives a little gasp, the dress so unexpectedly pretty.

"I only remember her wearing it once. We spent the day together, shopping at her store, maybe it was my birthday, I think, and then we had lunch in the Tea Room. I'd forgotten that. The store had a Tea Room."

"Then this is the dress she should wear," says Sybil. "So you can remember her in this dress, and remember that time. A funeral is for the living, Ray, not the dead."

He ponders this as if he's still a little frightened his mother will disapprove, his mouth working again. Sybil glances down at her fingers. It's none of her business. He has to decide this for himself.

"I'm not sure it'll fit her. She's so much smaller now."

"They can take care of that. They do that kind of thing all the time."

He lays the dress carefully on the bed. Smoothes out the skirt. "I didn't think she had this dress anymore. You know, my wife, ex-wife, is the one who helped her move in here. I was too busy."

"Your mother must have understood that."

"You're right. She did. If nothing else, she was proud of my success." He straightens up. "She's going to need shoes. The guy at the mortuary said a lot of people forget the shoes."

He turns back into the closet, comes up holding a pair of black orthopedic sandals.

"No," she says shaking her head. "Never."

"That's all she's got."

Sybil's stares at her feathery satin slippers. Too floozy. The rest of her shoes are like Louisa's, designed for comfort, not beauty. Then she remembers. "Hold on. I'll be right back." She pulls up the skirt of her silk robe so she can move faster and hurries outside. Feeling a little foolish and way too old to be streaking across the yard, she waves at Mars when he looks up puzzled and hollers "Hello," and heads into her garage at the back of her property.

It's dark inside and cold. Sybil flips on a light and starts shifting boxes, searching for the one labeled 'Jamie and Kids'. Amazing to Sybil how few belongings Jamie and her little family had. Toys, of course, a TV and VCR, and clothing. The furniture and most of the kitchen goods had been rented from Sybil; still she sent Mars German into the house once it was clear they had left, to bring out whatever could be salvaged against the day that Jamie would come back.

She's tried to find out who the girl's aunt is in Oregon. She's even reported to the police although Jamie and the kids are probably all right; she thinks someone besides herself should know the little family has disappeared off the face of the earth. The police detective was sympathetic, but optimistic. If a husband is difficult, then the wife doesn't want to be found. She wouldn't risk contacting anyone from her past. Sybil understands this, yet what if the police are wrong, and she is wrong, and Jamie's in trouble?

Jamie with her sad, quick smile. She has to be alright. Has to. And would she mind this gesture of Sybil's? This raiding of her shoes? Sybil doesn't think so. She opens the box and at its bottom, finds what she's looking for, a pair of white high heels with red leather detailing on the back.

Pulling herself up, back stiffening a little, Sybil smiles. She wants to see that look on Ray Renke's face again, the almost childlike remembrance in his eyes of a day well-spent with his mother. She knows that Louisa would be pleased, even though the old woman would always wave away any discussion of her son with the simple comment, "That boy. He deserves a better mother than me."

The Great Wall

by Sally-Anne Macomber

To: Milton Flaxmill, Red Cow Publishing
From: Trudy Polaris
Date: May 20, 2014 7:14 a.m.
Re: Cheese

Milton,

I swear, I did not know the fetta was Bulgarian!

You'd think someone would check these things. Get out their taste testers and taste the cheese for Bulgarianness.

Now of course, the Fetta Ambassadress job has blown up and most of the dairy producers in the Tyrol hate me! I walk down the street and see men with big moustaches, cowhorns dangling from their belts, glaring at me bog-eyed, their lips curling into high altitude snarls. And we're desperate for income during this tax break my husband is forcing us through and so things are not looking good.

I am fast discovering fetta is one of the least versatile cheeses around. Even with my superior culinary skills, it's just not possible to make fetta and couscous pancakes oh so light and fluffy this high above sea level.

BTW, any news on editing *Nuclear Fission in The Pyrénées*?

I confess, my book is the only thing that's keeping my mind on track. I have quite a bit more time on my hands again and I spend a lot of it just sitting on the cowskin sofa drinking *Edelweiss-schnaps* and thinking, now that the Fetta job has fallen through – plus, all the *dirndl* industry connections I had made have mysteriously disappeared, so hopes of a few extra € from catwalk modelling have been dashed too – so to quote some *Mitteleuropa* folk tales, things are looking grimm.

And every time I sit down at my computer to work through the *Nuclear Fission in The Pyrénées* manuscript myself, hoping inspiration will stab me, I look through the window and where once were snow-covered mountains, now stands a wailing wall of fetta. Local cheese retailers, once they discovered the truth, dumped their loads outside our Tyrolean hideaway. So our front yard smells suspiciously like what I think might be Bulgarian afterbirth.

And my new skill as a power-editor has derailed. Who needs a power-editor when after the goat milking is done, the day stretches out long and endless ...

And of course, whenever I milk a goat (and yes, they're still goats, they haven't changed back to cows again) the whole mess comes back to me and well, I need some good news.

How about I sneak out of here in the dead of night (to escape the glare of the tax border guards) and fly to Boston (I have a voucher for one and a half free flights with Bulgaria Air, and I can get a Bulgaria Air flight from Vienna to Boston via Sofia, which is just the break I deserve) so we can work on the book together?

I kind of need the money.

I could even have a t-shirt printed with *Boston or Bust* on the back. (Would *Nuclear Fission in The Pyrénées* across the front be a little crass?)

(Working out these flight details and wardrobe ideas are the only things holding me together at the moment, just in case you haven't realised the desperation of my desperation.)

Yours in the vain hope the sun is shining on a brighter tomorrow, tomorrow,

Trudy

Background

by Mandy Nicol

I thought Mum was joking when she came up with Persephone.

"You can't saddle a tiny Pomeranian with a name like Persephone," I'd said. But she didn't listen; this was Mum's new dog and she'd call it whatever she liked.

I call it Seph, which makes Mum purse her lips and dart her gaze away from me, in a Must You Always Find a Way to Annoy Me Nadia sort of way.

Mum got Seph after Peregrine was bitten by a snake last month. Mum said she knew Peregrine was going to die and she couldn't stand not having a dog around so we raced off to the local dog pound.

Of course Peregrine did survive so now we have two dogs.

I feel sorry for Peregrine. Mum is forever fussing over Seph, carrying her round the house like a handbag, letting her sit on her lap at meal times, giving her tidbits off her plate, "Look Nadia, Persephone likes your Apricot Chicken." Seph does nothing to deserve this attention, just jumps on all the furniture and trots around your feet nearly tripping you over whenever you move. She totally ignores commands unless there's something in it for her, like a piece of chicken, and if you take your eye off her outside she disappears so you end up wasting half your day searching sheds and paddocks to find her.

Faithful old Peregrine stays out of everybody's way. He's never growled at Seph, even when she eats his dinner right out of his bowl or lies on his blanket near the heater. I look at him now, lying under the dining room table, safe in the background, and I feel the pang of recognition.

Forget

by Margaret Bingel

At 6:13, the morning sun wakes Ned up, his eyes flash open, and he inhales deeply. Rising to greet the day, he stretches his arms out above his head. His elbows pop. Dr. Stanley had told him back in April that pops would happen, and not to worry, which is why he has no concerns with each new creak and crack that his body makes every morning.

Ned places his feet on the floor, and continues to stretch. His back cracks so hard his teeth vibrate. That's the good stuff, he thinks. He rocks his hips back and forth, swiveling his torso side to side, then bending further in each direction to wake up his muscles. His outpatient nurse told him that on days when he couldn't make it, Ned has to make extra-certain that these stretches and exercises are first order of business, to keep up muscle elasticity.

His nurse usually comes in on Mondays, Wednesdays and Fridays, but with the long holiday weekend coming up, he won't see his nurse until Wednesday. Ned has a strict routine of pilates and yoga (at least that's what it seems to him), but all Ned could think about while his nurse was telling him how to keep hydrated and eat plenty of lean protein was how he was going to drink beer and eat cheeseburgers. But right now, breakfast.

Ned ambles his way to the kitchen with only a slight stiffness to his gait. Dr. Stanley told him that it would take some time, but he has to be prepared for the possibility of never losing that limp. Here's a cane, Dr. Stanley told him, it could help you if you fall down. The cane sits in a corner, ignored.

After Ned puts bread into the toaster, he turns to the coffee pot and makes coffee. He likes Dr. Stanley, but like his mother, he feels that his doctor's trying to hold him back when all he wants to do is run forward. I'm a New Ned, he remembers telling Dr. Stanley. And New Ned doesn't hold back. The look on his mother's face when he said that was priceless, and just as he thinks about it, Ned scoops coffee right onto the counter. So he takes the coffee filter out of the pot, and with his hands brushes the grounds into the filter. Then putting the filter in the pot, he switches it on and returns to his toast.

Or, at least, there should be toast. The bread is sitting in the toaster and then Ned remembers that he didn't actually press the lever down. He shrugs his shoulders and presses the lever. But the bread pops up again. Ned stares at the toaster. And sees it isn't plugged in. Grabbing the cord, he points it toward the empty outlet, and sees the cord for the coffee pot lying on the counter, mocking him. So he shoves both cords into outlets and shuffles over to the table. Throwing himself into the chair, he runs his fingers through his hair, his nails scraping scalp, then digging deeper, and grunts.

It isn't the physical therapy that's holding him back. It's leaving keys in locks, forgetting to turn on the stove to cook, putting clothes on backwards. If he wasn't so young, Ned would think that he has Alzheimer's. He would call his mother for help, but he can't remember her number. Anyway, the New Ned is too strong for his mother.

The toaster pops up, and the smell of burned toast brings him back to reality.

Trees

by Darryl Price

Hey, Doc. Here's your ounce of blood.

Today I got taught how to draw some trees. I think I'm pretty good at it. All the pretty nurses touched my shoulder, so that's a good sign, right? I can draw trees that everybody likes. I must be okay. I mean would somebody who's not alright be able to draw a tree?

What is this? First grade? I want out of here.

I know you're the one with all the power. So let's make a deal. You said a story a day, right? Ok. Here's my next one.

Once upon a time there was a rabbit. This rabbit loved to smell purple flowers. One day while smelling those flowers, sitting in a field of the most beautiful purple flowers in the world, along comes a fox. The fox strides right up to the rabbit and says, I'm going to eat you. The rabbit starts to cry and says, but who will visit the flowers and sniff their beauty and take it all in and be thankful for it? Nobody, says the fox and he lunges at the rabbit, but the rabbit is quicker than he thinks and runs into the field of flowers that are all swaying crazily in the wind. Suddenly there's a kind of hum coming from the tops of the flowers and our little rabbit is suddenly, mysteriously lifted above their purple petals as if he's on a blanket. Meanwhile the fox sees what's going on and tries to jump up and catch the rabbit with his long hooked teeth, but no matter how high he jumps he just can't reach him. The rabbit is now smiling and rolling around on his back and flicking his whiskers at the clouds. All of a sudden there's a booming shot in the air and the sound of dogs barking and the fox shoots out of there like a red arrow never to be seen again. The rabbit softly drifts back down to the cool soft earth between all the flowers and sits very still until the hunters pass. The birds give him the signal that it's ok.

Not much of a story I guess. But it will have to do. I'm not a storyteller. I told you so.

I guess I am pretty good at trees though.

Why do I have to do all this art stuff?

I'm a free man. I just lost a girlfriend is all. That's not a crime – it's a tragedy. Let me go. Lift me up on your purple mountains majesty and let me go home.

Please.

Generosity

by Teresa Burns Gunther

Rachel and Stella finish their morning run, taking their time. It's Saturday. The fog is just beginning to burn off. Mrs. Franklin's already out in the narrow patch of garden that separates her home from Rachel's. The old woman is hunched in "work togs" digging at the roots of her roses. Stella barks, straining at her lead. Mrs. Franklin looks up and smiles.

"Hello precious!" Mrs. Franklin says in her soft Irish brogue. This greeting surprises Rachel who has only lived in the neighborhood a year and doesn't know her neighbor well. No one calls her *precious*.

"Yes … hello to you, too … Beautiful." Rachel feels silly saying this but she's working on her people skills and trying to be generous.

Mrs. Franklin laughs, a fluttering sound. "Oh. I was talking to your Stella," she says and scratches Stella's chin.

"Right. I'm joking with you," Rachel says, though she is not a joker. She hopes the flush of running will explain her burning cheeks.

"I bet you're wondering if I have something for you," Mrs. Franklin says to Stella, reaching into her pocket. She pulls out a cookie, her fingers are red, cracked, her lips chapped. Rachel makes a note to pick up moisturizer from

Macy's when she's shopping later. Her resolution for May is: *be generous.*

Rachel can see the woman's pale scalp through her wispy cloud of white hair and feels a fierce desire to protect this brittle woman. Stella whimpers. Rachel tightens her hold on the leash. Mrs. Franklin has cats. Rachel is glad they are indoor pets since Stella's exuberance for life extends to taking the same from small creatures like birds, cats and the Aussies' rabbit, though it was in fact already dead.

"Be polite, Stella," Rachel says. "Sit."

"How do you greet an old lady then?" Mrs. Franklin says. Stella sits and raises her paw to the liver-spotted hand. "It's a fine dog you have here," she tells Rachel and stands, one hand on Stella's head. Everyone else is afraid of Stella, though she wouldn't hurt anyone, without provocation. "How are you getting on?"

"Fine," Rachel says. "Except the Aussies keep complaining about Stella."

"Why?" Mrs. Franklin's wrinkled face folds into a frown.

"She barks too much."

Mrs. Franklin leans out to peer down the street where Joyce directs her beanpole husband as he washes their car. "She's a prickly one, is she?"

"Maybe so much time with manure and veg has taken a toll." Rachel taps her temple.

Mrs. Franklin considers this. "Well, I say your Stella can bark all she likes. Keeps the riffraff away." Stella rubs her flank against the woman's leg as if she understands. "We single ladies," Mrs. Franklin says raising her salt and pepper brows, "can't be too careful. Besides, I don't hear her bark."

"Maybe you should have your hearing checked."

"What's that, dear?"

§

In the afternoon, Rachel tours the glass cosmetics counters at Macy's. The Lancôme saleswoman follows her, smiling with white teeth and plumpy lips. She compliments Rachel on her beautiful skin, her *lovely* summer dress. "How can I help you today?"

Rachel sets her shopping bag on the counter. "I just need some free samples of moisturizer. For dry skin." The smile disappears. "It's for a little old lady, a neighbor. She has terribly chapped skin."

"How nice of you." The saleswoman smirks, fussing with a silk scarf wrapped in a complicated knot at her neck. "And … buying a whole jar would be just … too, too much?" Her lashes are so caked with mascara Rachel blinks.

"Well," Rachel shrugs, "these are free." Then catching her meaning, adds, "I'm just trying to be helpful." She resents the accusation. "Besides, she might not like it. What if she's allergic?"

"And I'm guessing you don't want to splurge on anything for yourself," the woman says with an exaggerated sigh as she sets a few samples on the counter. Rachel has been practicing keeping her mouth shut in moments like this but the woman's snotty tone and pinched face, as if she's suffering a terrible smell, sets her off.

"What do you care what I do or don't buy?" Rachel asks. "It's not like it's your stuff. And no, I'm not going to *splurge* on anything. Because you. are. rude."

"*I'm* rude?" The saleswoman is warming to her cause as other shoppers draw near clutching designer bags, eyes shifting between them, all curiosity. "You come in here, waste my time and only want free handouts and then you call *me* rude?"

"I'm just trying to do a nice – oh, never mind." Rachel sweeps the samples from the counter with a flourish, grabs her shopping bag, spins on her heel, swinging her bag so that it smacks a blind man with a cane and sends him flying. A collective gasp echoes the blind man's cry. Rachel drops down beside him, smoothing his jacket, helping him up. "I'm sorry. I didn't see you." That's when the saleswoman yells for someone to call security. Rachel retrieves the man's cane lost in the fall. His eyes are hidden behind dark glasses. "I guess you didn't see me either." She helps the blind man to a stool as the curious onlookers scatter, though the saleswoman is trying to spin the mishap into a crime.

Rachel tries to explain the situation to the blue-suited manager who arrives with a uniformed officer on his heels. Everyone starts shouting at once. "It was an accident," Rachel shouts loudest and everyone freezes. The blind man assures everyone he's fine. The guard takes Rachel's name and she's free.

She races out through the cloying haze of perfume to Union Square, nearly tripping over a homeless man camped on the sidewalk. She's so flustered that when her phone rings she answers without checking caller ID. It's her cousin, Susie, announcing she's coming for a visit, which means she's unemployed again. "God no!" Rachel says and hangs up. At her car a ticket waits on her windshield.

After her terrible day, Rachel stops by Mrs. Franklin's. There's no answer to her knock. She's about to leave when the door opens a crack.

"Who's there?" Mrs. Franklin calls from behind the door.

"It's Rachel. Next door?"

"Oh, yes." She unlatches the door and swings it wide. She beams at Rachel who isn't accustomed to eliciting joy. "Come in!"

"I have to go home." Rachel shivers. The fog has rolled its thick blanket back over the city, blocking the sun. "I just stopped by to give you something."

Mrs. Franklin tilts her head. "Yes?" She waits, hands clasped to her belly. Rachel searches her shopping bag but now doesn't know how to explain the "gift".

"Here." She holds the samples in her hand. "I got these for you when I was shopping. For dry skin. I thought," she hesitates, "you could ... like them." She blushes again. Thanks to that saleswoman, the slender packets of cream feel small. And cheap.

"Aren't you the kind one? Won't you come in? I'm just making tea."

Rachel hesitates. "I can't."

"Oh sure. It's Saturday. A date is it?" Mrs. Franklin asks with a mischievous smile.

"No. Just Stella," Rachel explains. "She needs to get out."

Mrs. Franklin's smile falls. "Oh. Of course."

After her father's visit two months before Rachel can't stop thinking about him asking: "Where are your friends?" And "Do you ever go out of your way for *them*?" At first she dismissed it as a dig because she'd refused to let him stay with her. Now it dogs her. She'd gone out of her way for Gail, her officemate, last month when she was practicing patience but it backfired. Now Gail has befriended her neighbor, Joyce, who hates her and Stella. Rachel's beginning to think Stella may be her best and only friend.

Mrs. Franklin's door closes, then pops back open. She calls after Rachel. "Thank you for the creams. You're a fine colleen. You tell your mother she raised you proper."

Rachel stands on the sidewalk stunned, wishing her father could hear, wishing her boss could hear, and Gail, and Joyce, and the saleswoman at Saks, wondering if she should tell Mrs. Franklin that her name's Rachel, not Colleen, and that her mother no longer knows her. She can hear Stella barking but now, doesn't want to leave.

"My day's been a train wreck, Mrs. Franklin. I could come later? After I deal with Stella?"

"Now that's a grand idea." Mrs. Franklin's smile picks up, bigger and brighter. "We'll have a cocktail and you can tell me all about it. I'll snap myself up a bit and find us something special. And bring Stella along," she says as a cat appears, purring and wrapping itself around her legs.

Morgana Malone and the Riddle of the Sands of Time

by Matt Potter

The sand thwumps out of the upturned jar. Well, it would, except it's not sand.

"This is not sand," Ludmilla says, looking down at the coloured crystals spreading across the table. Her dull brown hair streaked with grey frames her face in a lank way that says, *I don't know what else to do with it and who cares anyway?!*

I pat my own hair – blown-about orange bob with ever-widening grey-brown re-growth striped across the top – and look down at the table too. The table that … I don't know … but when I read her small ad in the *Psychic News* I thought would be flat and probably smooth, perhaps metal or at least Laminex but not this pitted old wooden thing with dips and knots and channels in the grain.

I place the jar down on the table with a glassy clink. The pink straw resting beside it rolls toward me and settles in a crack.

"Well, no," I say, digging the straw out with my finger. "But I *did* get it *near* the beach. And *I* bought it, it wasn't someone else who bought it, it was me, with my money. I picked it up off the shelf and, you know …" I would keep talking but I think my voice has floated off down the street and across the Southern Ocean.

I pick the straw up.

Ludmilla sits back in her chair, shoulders wheezing against the vinyl. As she opens her mouth I see her teeth are a dull beige.

"But I am a sand reader," she says, crossing her arms under her cavernous cleavage so her breasts spill over her pale forearms. "I need the sand to be reading your fortune and this is just …" – her cheeks fill with air and she exhales, her breath slow and small across the table but direct against my face, and I smell garlic and onion and what could be borscht: maybe that's her power, really, windpower, not this sand reading stuff – "… it is not the correct sand."

Well, yes, no, I agree, it's not sand. It's a jar of bath salts really, originally bought with the dark colours layered at the bottom – grape and purple and lilac – then up to the pinks – shocking and coral and flamingo – and then baby pink and cream and white … but then I unscrewed the top and spooned out the first two layers and shook it up like a martini, shaking and shaking and shaking and then I stirred the first two layers back in with the same spoon.

(I was given those bath salts in a Secret Santa three Christmases ago.)

(And that shaking was the most exercise I had all day.)

I put the straw back on the table.

(Walking out the front door has been an exercise in discipline I currently don't have much of. It's safer to sit inside in the dark. And I have a lot of time now since I stopped working as the admin junior at Grigor's psychiatry practice, up-managing Zebadie the porn star / receptionist. So I just sit in the dark and think. And thinking is a good way to *not* spend money when you don't have a job.)

"But it is all *focked*," Ludmilla says, breasts bobbing in indignation on her forearms. "I am supposed to be giving you a straw and we both put on some glasses for protecting our eyes and then you blow on the sand and make some pretty pictures and I interpret them for your future but –" and she throws her hands in the air so her breasts thwop back against her stomach "– this is some pretty pictures in a bottle and is not some sand you get from your favourite spot on the beach that has some meanings in your life." She crosses her arms again – this time, *over* her breasts – and pushing out her bottom lip, she breathes out, her straggly grey-brown fringe fluttering against her forehead. Which I now see has a large red pimple with a bulbous yellow head glistening in the middle of it.

"They were in a jar," I say, eyes popping, grasping for the truth amongst this psychic mess, "it's a *jar*, Ludmilla, it's not *focked*. A jar." And I stab a free spot on the table with my index finger. "A *jar* is not a *bottle*. And a jar is not *focked* by definition because it's a *jar*. A *bottle* is *tapered*" – my hands flash through the air outlining a tapering bottle – "and has a small *opening* at the *top* but a *jar* is the same circumference all the way up, usually." And again, my hands carve the air creating an impromptu jar. "Like a wheat *silo* except made of *glass* and a lot *smaller*."

I don't know why I'm *emphasising* certain *words*.

I sit back against the chair and my shoulders whisper against the vinyl.

Actually, I don't know why I'm doing anything.

"Can't you interpret bath salts?" I ask, my voice thin and wan and nothing. "I can blow on the bath salts with the straw and make *prettier* pictures."

Ludmilla leans forward and, breasts now resting on the table, sinks her chin into her hand.

"But my talent is reading the sand that has some special reason for you," Ludmilla says, "and since you telephoned me and saying my ex-husband is giving me the sack and now I have no job and my life is in the toilets and I need some hope."

I look down at the sand, I mean the bath salts, and they're all mixed into a murky pinky sugary brown so, if you were drunk enough, you could spoon them into your mouth then pretend you were having a diabetic episode.

"But if you cannot make a trip to the beach with a bucket and a ... a ... you know, a *dig dig* thing then ... to save your life and to get some directions then your life is *focked* and I cannot help you if you cannot help yourself."

It comes from somewhere, I don't know where, but a smile appears at the corner of my mouth. "Oh, you mean *fucked*?" I say. But the way I say it, I say 'fecked'. Like Ludmilla would say if she were imitating my Australian accent.

"Focked, fecked, fooked," she chants, "whenever, it is all the same for you."

"Yes," I say. And picking up the straw, I put it to my lips and blow hard, covering Ludmilla's vast continental shelf with my focked future.

O

by Gary Percesepe

I'm in a bar when I butt-dial my wife, or rather my ex-wife. It isn't the first time.

Jesus, she says. Take the phone out of your back pocket. Fucking Christ. This is embarrassing.

I know. What are you doing?

I'm working at this ridiculous summer church camp upstate your mother talked me into. Today I walked in on two girls in the bottom bunk bed going at it. From North fucking Carolina, can you believe it? Billy Graham country.

I picture two fourteen year olds, their front flats grinding together, lying head to toe, the dark haired one's narrow foot grazing the pin shaped nipple of the blonde girl, the blonde's chlorine-faded blue swim suit pulled down around her ankles.

What'd you do? I ask. Perfect pitch.

I called *Hustler* for a contract. What the fuck do you think I did? I said move the fuck over.

Savannah divorced me, citing irreconcilable differences, but we never differed on the sex. We fucked every day, more as we got closer to the paper signing at the courthouse. It's a mystery.

You remember when we beat off to *Hustler* when you were pregnant?

Gawd. I couldn't keep you off of me when I was pregnant. I bought you those to calm you down.

Didn't work, I guess.

The thing about these two girls, they wouldn't stop. They were rocking that bunk after I left, all trying to be discreet. Jesus.

A new world, I say.

Savannah used to volunteer as a mom helper during recess. She was politely spoken to after she let one of the boys, a twelve year old, take off his shirt for her. She told me later she liked the shape of his nipple under his tee shirt, it was a perfect dime. Later, when she was headed to her car after school one day the kid caught up to her and asked for a lock of her hair. Savannah yanked the ends off a few strands of her French braid and handed them over. Knock yourself out, she said.

Are you getting any, Savannah asks.

You mean tonight? I say.

Tonight, tomorrow.

There's a poet I'm interested in. But she's in Oregon.

Ha! Fifty thousand women who'd fuck you in town and you wanna hook up with a poet in Oregon! That's perfect. God, I love you.

I sip at my beer. The barmaid looks over and asks with her eyes am I OK? She's got some art on her chest that looks interesting, a series of concentric circles in delicate green ink that looks like a bull's eye. She refills me. Last week I fucked her up against the wall of the bar at three am. She presented her ass, slippery and canted at an interesting angle. I told Savannah afterwards on the phone. Another butt call on the drive home.

Our relationship should be reported to the Guinness people, I say.

Tell me about your poetess, Savannah says.

She's got a new book out, written from the point of view of a teenage boy, I say. He jacks off in the back of the bus

113

on the way to school. He covers up with his book bag but the driver sees him. I listened to a podcast of her reading this poem at her book launch and she giggled when she got to that part. She said, I always wanted to do that.

Ooh, I like her, Savannah says. I'd fuck her just for that. What's she look like?

She's Irish, with big brown puppy eyes and short blonde hair like yours. She's skinny with no hips or butt and she likes to pose with a gun on Facebook. She's got a big O tattoo on her left arm.

Mmmmm, Savannah says.

Don't get any ideas.

Look, I gotta go, Savannah says.

I hear somebody in the background saying c'mon, willya. I take a long drink from my beer and rest my head on my arm on the bar.

Are you there?

Yes, I say.

I'm worried about you. Are you sure you're OK tonight?

I sit up on my stool. I signal the girl for another beer.

Sure, I'm fine. Hey, sure. Sorry about the butt call. Won't happen again.

She clicks off and I imagine the poet girl brushing her teeth in the bathroom of her studio apartment. There's a cat to get past. I move in behind her and reach around her narrow waist. She quivers and I let her go, then reach around and take the toothbrush in my left hand and finish the job. She spits white into the sink and I wipe her mouth with my outstretched finger. I run the water in the bath and bend her over from the waist until her hair is under the stream of hot water. She drops to her knees. I apply the shampoo generously, moving my fingers through her hair, pressing deep into her scalp, holding her head under the water until she moans and turns around and pulls me underneath her. I fall to the floor by the base of the tub and look up at those brown eyes. She makes her fingers into a gun. Bang, she says.

Samford's Big Race

by Nathaniel Tower

Sweat rolls down his naked ass crack as Samford stands at the starting line, waist bent and arms cocked and ready to run. He doesn't know why he's sweating when the race hasn't started yet. Perhaps it's nerves. Or maybe it's a sign that late May is turning into summer already.

A sudden breeze tickles Samford's exposed genitals. To keep from getting aroused, Samford looks around at the crowd. They are cheering, not necessarily for him. Still, he revels in the cheers for a moment, contemplating the journey that brought him here. He'd never been much for athletics before, and now he has a chance to win.

Samford has been training for the clone Olympics for the past month, ever since the clone police took him captive. His training hasn't been voluntary. In fact, he's been told that he must win or his body will be deactivated. He's not sure how this works. He was always under the impression that clones were just as real as flesh-born humans. Maybe they had said "decapitated."

The gun fires, snapping Samford back to the track. Immediately he's four strides behind the pack. His bare feet slap against the rubberized track, but the sound of his balls smacking back and forth on his pasty thighs drowns them out. Even the roar of the crowd is no match for the banging from his swinging sack.

He hasn't worn clothes for a month, but somehow the sun's rays have not darkened him. He's just as pale as he ever was. Maybe even paler.

He forgets about his pallor and sprints hard until he catches the pack. Then he settles in, the rhythmic sound of more than a dozen ballsacks swinging back and forth in unison causing a strange sense of calm.

Hanging on to the pack as they make their way around the track for the first lap, his chest heaves as he struggles for adequate oxygen. For a moment, he panics, convinced his training hasn't been enough. He tries to remember the tips his coach gave him, but his mind is blank. Devoid of any guidance or sound strategy, he sprints to the front of the pack.

He crosses the line to complete the first lap. The crowd roars his name, and he glances back to see his fifteen-stride lead. Way out front, he is suddenly confident. His shoulders drop and all parts of his body move like an automaton. For the first time in a month, he's happy to be a clone.

"Sam-ford! Sam-ford!" the crowd cheers. He pushes his body harder, his stride opening longer as his quads and lungs begin to burn. He wonders why they are rooting for him, why they even know his name.

"And Samford has broken free and is on record pace!" an announcer yells over a cackling speaker. The excitement pushes Samford harder, and he charges around to finish the second lap with a forty-meter lead. Two laps to go. Although the pace is really starting to tire his body, he continues to push, trying to run faster and faster. He has no idea what the record is, but he plans to set it right now. Why hadn't he taken up running in his younger days? Then he remembers that he doesn't even remember if he had younger days.

The third lap is a blur, and Samford can't hear the slapping of his balls anymore. He looks down for a second and sees they have shriveled into tiny raisin pouches and can no longer thwack against his legs.

As he crosses the line to enter the final lap, he glances back and can't see any competitors on the home stretch. He knows he cannot lose with such an enormous lead, but he does not slow down, even with the fear that people will accuse him of being a cyborg or some other superhuman entity. Clones shouldn't be any better than the humans they are cloned from.

He's halfway around the track on the final lap, burning past clones still on their third lap, when the sirens wail. It sounds like an air raid, but Samford does not stop running.

"Clear the stadium now!" the announcer calls.

Samford passes five more clones until he enters the homestretch. For the first time, he sees the large clock near the finish line. The big green numbers tell him he has been running for three minutes and twelve seconds. His eyes widen. Even with his limited knowledge of track and field, he knows he is on pace for a world record. He knows he must finish.

"Clones, get off the track!" the announcer says.

Samford keeps running. He will not be denied his glory.

He is less than ten strides from the finish line when the the clock display disappears. With all tangible signs of glory gone, the pain suddenly overwhelms his body.

"Get off the track now!" the announcer yells.

Fire now roars in his lungs. Samford takes two more strides before his body crumples to the rubber surface. A rifle crack echoes from above. Samford's body rolls off the track and onto the grassy infield. He has only a few seconds to contemplate whether the sharp pain in his gut is from the run, the fall, or a bullet, and then all colors fade and he lies motionless in a fetal position, his shriveled penis and balls tucked between his pale legs.

We Have Company

by Kimberlee Smith

We have company. I thought my husband Dean and I would be in limbo, alone, for eternity. It's not that I don't love him, but the past few months have been like the two of us are stranded on a deserted island. Without the island.

Today, May 28, a woman about my mum Maybell's age, late '40s, early '50s, comes along out of nowhere and says, "I'm Doreen and I'm just passing through. Not hanging around here. Nope." She points up like she's poking the sky, trying to get its attention.

"Oh really? And where do you think you're going?" I ask. Dean feels closer, in a show-of-solidarity kind of way.

"Yeah. We've been here a little while, and hate to be the bearer of bad news. Obviously not the *worst* news you've ever gotten because it seems you know you died. You do know, don't you?" says Dean. He can be rhetorical when he's fired up.

Doreen scratches at what I imagine was recently her waist, maybe where her knickers pinched her. Instead, her hand slices right through her midsection and her torso kind of gapes open. She doesn't seem to notice she went right through her old body and has a flat palm rummaging around her innards. There's no blood trickling out; it's all gone.

"Sorry, Doreen, but this is it. The end," I say with a wince.

Doreen doesn't answer right away because she notices her hand is inside her sternum and instead of seeming horrified she looks embarrassed; her eyes darting all around and she mimics, I guess without knowing, what it's like to be out of breath. Wiping her brow as if she's sweating, but she's not. She's dry as a bone. Dusty already. Have you heard when a person loses a limb they feel the ghost of it for a long time, as if it's still there? I believe that's what's happening to her, but from the inside out.

"Oh, dear. This is, well, not something to share now, is it?" she whispers.

Dean seems pleased that he might have stumped her. He's got a ruddy tone like he did when he was alive; color fills him and the brightness of sunshine fills the old bog-water color he just was. I can tell when he's mischievous on purpose, and since he joined me here he hasn't had anyone's chain to yank but mine.

But the flush of color doesn't stop at ruddy. When he gets cheeky with me, I can see the flames that killed him lick him from the inside, they flicker and flash and there's a stench of burned flesh. But he reacts like he's just got hives like he used to get when he was in his body and he ate too many tomatoes. He has no idea that fire has stayed with him.

"Of course I know," says Doreen, turning indignant as she bends her elbows akimbo and tries to settle her fists at her hips. They pass right through her.

"You think _you_ wouldn't know if a seven-meter saltwater crocodile had you for tea?"

"Really? You think that's more of an eye-opener to recognizing you're a goner, than say, being trapped alone in a plane that slammed into the ground, and being incinerated to ash? Try _my_ kind of death. You'd be praying for a saltie to split you in half."

Dean is losing it. I cannot believe there's a 'You Think That's Bad' contest between these two when we haven't seen – literally – another soul for months?

I have to break up the pissing match. I don't know how to leave, and even if I did, where would I be going?

"Pardon me," I say in a voice that really isn't my voice at all, it's more of a rumble zinging with electricity, like what you feel when thunderheads are about to crack. "I've about had it with you both. Dead is dead. So enough."

They both look like guilty children who need good spankings; they're scowling and pursing their lips. I'd like to slug them both. Three is a crowd. This is not working.

And how fucking long is she going to hang around? I was hoping for company, but her intrusion has thrown our balance completely *off*. I'm curious now. I can't wait to find out how she's meeting up with her family and I hope it's soon. I've heard enough of their yammering.

I'm here, too. Nobody seems to give a shit that I died. Wait, that's not right. My mum gives a shit. And our baby only knows me dead; a dead mummy is the only kind my bubbie knows.

"Mine was by snakebite," I say, interrupting the silence. Lightning cleaves the sky. It happens with frequency – lightning and thunder that I first feel, and then my voice changes – when I get emotionally charged. I am not surprised that the energy that builds up in me causes an electrical storm of epic proportions.

When the shock passes through, *boom!* I feel alive again for a moment, tingly and flushed, as if that were possible. The storm leaves the confines of me and explodes into our afterworld, and then it's gone.

Doreen doesn't notice it. Dean hasn't ever, either. It might just be me and I'm going to keep this crazy, amazing secret to myself. I don't feel like sharing anything with them.

"I went first. Dean, a couple months later."

"It's a huge inconvenience. Terribly sad for the family, I imagine," says Doreen.

Dean and I chime in together and our expressions overlap. It's a habit. "Indeed." "Absolutely." "No doubt about that."

"Not much family left," says Dean. Now he is pale gray, like an oyster. Almost opaque but vaguely translucent. That's what happens when he's sad. He's like a human mood ring.

"Our daughter, our only child, Etheline Margaret, was born immediately after I was pronounced dead. The doctors Caesared her right out of me as soon as they could. I believe they had to save the baby, because they weren't too hopeful about saving me. Too much toxicity from the venom, right babe?" I say to Dean.

"Yep. That's true. I was there. Oh, our sweet little bub. A heartbreaking shame you weren't able to hold her, even once. We missed you so much. That's the worst part," he says, falling into me like a wounded flower. It feels and smells like a thousand jacaranda blossoms, as light as a silk shroud.

When either one of us becomes melancholy or nostalgic this magical thing happens. And I'm certain it's on account of the jacaranda trees Dean planted for me as a Christmas present, our last Christmas. And our first spent in our new home. It was the best time of our lives, and certainly the best time since.

There's a shower of intoxicating jacaranda perfume and petals whorling all around us. They were my favorite flowers. They *are* my favorite flowers.

It's as if Doreen isn't here at all right now. She doesn't feel or see or smell this, either, the same way she didn't have any perception to the storm. I can just tell. It's a phenomenon too spectacular to ignore.

"But you know, babe, I'm always with her," I say. We call each other that. *Babe.* It's another habit of ours.

"Holy. Motherofgod. Seriously?" says Doreen. The flowers have all blown away, but they'll come back.

"Dead serious," I say, and we all laugh a little awkward laugh about the inside joke. I can be funny sometimes, and right now is a time that calls for it.

When the laughter dies down – see? I just punned death again! – there's more awkwardness, but it's in the form of silence.

"She was born January 14. Exactly a month before our second wedding anniversary," I say.

"You were married on Valentine's Day?" asks Doreen, like it was an odd thing to do.

"Of course! It's the most romantic day of the year," says Dean, like it's something she should consider as fact.

"So who's taking care of the bub now?" asks Doreen.

"My mum," I say, "it's just the two of them now, no other family to speak of."

"Well that explains why you two are still farting around here," says Doreen.

"Meaning what?" asks Dean. His head snaps towards her and smoke billows out of his ears. For real.

"Meaning you're not moving on because you're keeping a watch over your little girl. Mind you, you can go meet your maker any time you're inclined. You're obviously not ready," says Doreen. "I'm going to see what all the fuss about the pearly gates is about. And reunite with my husband Hugo. Also my sister Laralee and our mum and dad. I was the last one left."

"What makes you think you can?" I ask.

Dean doesn't give her time to answer, "She told you, this is the end of the line. There's nowhere else to go." He swings his fists in the air like he's fighting a cloud of rabid bats.

"You're wrong as wrong gets. The reason you're still here in nowhere land is because you don't want to leave. You could leave whenever you like. You're denying that you can," says Doreen as she tries to tuck her blouse back into her pants, but instead she tucks it behind her pelvis and pulls it out, cusses to herself, and tries again. She does this a number of times until I am bored watching her.

"How are *you* an expert on moving out of here?" asks Dean.

"You haven't come across anyone else here, have you?" challenges Doreen, as if she knows the answer.

Dean and I look at each other. She's got a point.

And then she tells us how she knows.

"I been here before."

Personal

by Vanessa Weibler Paris

~~Hi, my name is Jim. My friends call me Slim Jim.~~

~~Hi, my name is Jim. I would love to meet a lady of any size or appearance~~

~~Hi, my name is James. You can call me Jim. My friends all do.~~

~~Single white male. Down to earth and easygoing. New to online dating. Not into playing games.~~

~~Call me Jimshmael. Some years ago — never mind how long precisely —~~

~~I enjoy going out and partying, but I also love curling up at home with that special someone.~~

~~My name begins with a J. I am a riddle wrapped in a mystery inside an enigma. I am a chicken placed inside a duck slid within a turkey. I am puff pastry. An onion. Lasagna. Spanakopita.~~

~~Okay, I don't know what to write, so how about if I just give you my name, and maybe if you have a dad named Jim or a brother named Jim or maybe a good male friend named Jim, but a platonic friend not one who you used to date and are kind of secretly still hung up or is still hung up on you, then maybe you'd want to maybe~~

~~[different less stupid opening] long walks on the beach, wine by the fire, pina coladas~~

~~Hi, I'm Jim! I don't mind if you're way too fat if you don't mind if I'm way too skinny.~~

~~Hi, I'm Jim! I don't mind if you're big and beautiful if you don't mind if I'm skinny and ugly.~~

~~Hi, I'm Jim! I don't mind if you're [something that means big but doesn't insult them—ask coworkers for ideas] if you don't mind if I'm way too skinny.~~

~~Someone [look up who this was] once said that beauty is in the eye of the beholder. [make joke about bumper sticker, "beauty is in the eye of the beer holder?" maybe not?]~~

~~My name is James. Hey, that rhymes! Kind of.~~

~~SWM seeks SWF. Will you be the olive to my toothpick?~~

~~Jack Sprat seeks wife~~

~~Jack Sprat seeks companion to lick the platter clean~~

~~Jack Sprat seeks companion to enjoy a nice meal of varying caloric~~

~~If I could rearrange the alphabet, I'd put 'I' and 'U' together~~

~~Did it hurt when you fell from heav~~

Jim is the nicest guy we know. Who is "we"? There are three of us, all women, all at least 20 years his senior, and Jim works in our department and eats lunch with us every day.

How is Jim nice?

When Linda's mom died, he spent his Saturday driving four hours each way just to attend the funeral.

When Darlene's husband walked out on her and she was having an especially down night, he brought over three chick flick movies, a bottle of wine and a half-gallon of ice cream, and hung out until they were done with all five. And then he waited 'til she was asleep before leaving.

When Barbara got marked down on her annual review for not being good at spreadsheets, he came over every night for a week to coach her along.

And when his best friend Dougie went through chemo, he sat there in that room with him for hours, distracting him from the dry hot air and the drip of the line and the occasional stifled sob with round after round of pinochle.

Jim is the nicest guy we know.

There's a lot more to Jim than being nice – in fact, it's far from the most interesting thing about him – but that's for you to learn.

Do you want to?

Dinner Date

by Joanne Jagoda

Why can't it be 3:10? Friday is the slowest day, and it's stuffy in here. We almost never need air conditioning in San Francisco, but I wish we had it today. The kids smell sour from gym class and they are restless. Every damn tick of the clock sounds like a time bomb.

"Darren, no talking. Just settle down and finish your test."

I want it to be night already and to be with David … yummy, yummy David. He wouldn't tell me where we're going. Some *gourmet* restaurant, and I'm supposed to "dress up." Dressing up with Paul meant we were going to the Sizzler. I had a reason to go into that boutique on 24th St. which I passed a million times oohing over the clothes in the window. I found the perfect black knit dress, short with a ruffly skirt. This feels like my prom tonight, with my new dress, and I'm splurging and getting my nails and hair done after school. Last week the girls went to their prom. Cassie got asked at the last minute by one of the boys in her group of the straight 'A' kids and Robin went with a boy from another school. Lillian insisted on taking them shopping for their prom dresses even though I wanted to do it. You can't say no to their grandmother who thinks she is the queen of fashion. Finally lunch. There's the bell.

"Turn in your tests."

"Anne, you heading to the lunchroom?"

"Hi, Tracy. I'll walk with you."

"Anne, let's grab this table. Do you want some bad coffee?"

"Sure. Black is fine. Thanks."

"What is it about you Anne that's different? Your hair? New makeup? You're sure smiling a lot. Are you getting laid? Spill the beans."

"Tracy, very funny. But … well … you're right. I did meet someone. And we're *not* sleeping together. Not yet anyway."

"Cute Anne. You're blushing. I knew it, I knew it. Spill. Tell me everything."

"His name is David Lewis, and we met by chance at the Fairmont Hotel. I had been stood up by an online blind date. That's a whole other story. Anyway, I was having a Cosmo by myself at the bar. This really cute guy sits next to me. He gave me his card before he left, and I finally got around to calling him. We met up at Pier 39 last month."

"Don't stop. I want to hear more."

"I was a wreck half-expecting him to not show, but he was there waiting for me. I have to tell you he's cute; tall, blue eyes and dark hair to his collar. He had on a leather jacket, and has an adorable English accent. I *love* his accent. We took the ferry boat to Alcatraz, but it was cold that morning with a vicious wind, and we couldn't sit outside."

"Go *on*, Anne. This is getting good."

"We huddled inside the tour boat watching the rolling waves and sipping hot chocolate. David is easy to talk to. He wanted to know about the girls and my teaching and everything about Paul. He lost his wife Sybil to breast cancer. I felt so bad for him. His eyes filled with tears when he spoke about her."

"What does he do?"

"He has an international company, something with computers, and came here to open an office south of Market. We loved the tour of Alcatraz. Back at the wharf, we had crab cocktails and shared a loaf of French bread. The most fun was hopping on the cable car hanging on outside, battered by the wind. We had dinner at Kuleto's and chocolate sundaes at Ghiradelli Square. He insisted on paying for everything. By 8pm I had to get back to the girls. I felt like Cinderella. He gave me the sweetest peck on the cheek and a big hug and promised to call me soon which he did by the next day."

"The next day? Ohhhh Ann. He sounds perfect. Tell me he has a brother. Have you been seeing him a lot?"

"We've been going out every weekend. Long hikes in Golden Gate Park, touring the de Young Museum, strolling at Ocean Beach, seeing foreign films in the Castro and trying all types of food, from Szechuan to Ethiopian."

"Have the girls met him?"

"Not yet. After my blind date disaster, I didn't want to say anything about going out with him. They thought I was meeting an old friend from college but noticed I was spending more time getting ready than usual. It didn't take much for Cassie and Robin to figure out what was going on. They're very sneaky and found my emails to David on my laptop because they know my password. I was pissed at first, but I know they worry about me.

"After a month of sneaking around, I sat them down at one of our 'family' meetings to tell them I met someone. They acted surprised at first but couldn't stop kicking each other under the table and told me they knew. They had even named him *Dude*. The girls wanted to hear everything about him."

"There's the bell. When are you seeing him again?"

"Tonight we're going out and he wouldn't tell me where."

"That sounds romantic I want to hear about it on Monday."

Oh my gosh, the bell is about to ring. Finally this day is done. "Turn in your tests and have a good weekend. No homework. You don't have to yell so loud. Get out of here!"

They love weekends without homework. I'm glad I got through today. I better hurry. My hair appointment is at 3:30. I am going to have work to do to correct these damn tests over the weekend since I wasted the whole day daydreaming. I'm glad the girls won't be home tonight. I'm not ready to introduce David to them.

I'm going over my spreadsheet again. Everything has to be perfectly timed. I hope my employers got the message from my email this morning to get off my goddamn back. I couldn't have said it any plainer. This operation can't be rushed. I need this job to go perfectly. I'm going to make enough money to get out of this business. When I get my fat cheque I'm taking off for good.

No one down on the street, but I feel like I'm being followed. I'm usually the one doing the spying. They must not trust me and have someone watching me.

Looking forward to wining and dining Anne. We're going to Gary Danko. Perfect place ... elegant but hip and not too stuffy. She'll love it. And no woman could resist me in this brown ultra-suede sport coat and dark blue shirt. I'm such a handsome devil. I'll splash a drop of that expensive cologne from Barney's, subtle but sexy. This is a slow dance ... the long kisses, a few gropes of her perfect bum, and caresses of her nicely endowed body. Too bad Anne, my darling, in another life I might have gone for you. I've never been able to stick with one woman with the kind of nasty work I do travelling around the world. Taking her to bed is the next step to pull her in. I'll suggest a wine country weekend next month. The kidnapping will happen before Cassie leaves for university in September.

Grandpa George will be deciding the fate of his precious granddaughter. To get her back alive, he is going to have to turn over the schematics for the advanced missile blocker system, Project Octopus, developed by his Silicon Valley company, which can capture and destroy missiles with uncanny accuracy and from a much further distance than the previous Iron Dome technology. My employers will stop at nothing to get those blueprints. That's why they hired me. I'm the best, and I'm ruthless. And I want my payday.

I'm glad I ditched that crappy rental for this silver BMW M3 convertible. This is the first time I've picked her up at her home, but she doesn't know I've been in her pretty little house putting in my cameras and listening devices.

She must have been standing near the door. She opened it before I could ring. She is stunning. The only thing real about me is my smile when I see her sexy body.

"Anne, you look amazing."

"Thanks David. You're not too bad yourself. OK, I'm dying to know. Where we going?"

"Sorry, m'lady. Can't tell you yet. But I thought we'd have a glass of champagne first. I brought my favourite Veuve Clicquot."

"I don't have champagne glasses. I'll get us some wine glasses."

Ahh, the girls' photos are here on the mantel. Pretty things aren't they. I'd hate to have to hurt Cassie.

"Your girls are lovely. Cassie looks just like you; I'm assuming Robin takes after your late husband. May I propose a toast Anne? To a wonderful evening, no change that ... to many wonderful evenings."

Visit to the Temple

by h. l. nelson

Dear Diary,

This has been the craziest twenty-four hours of my life. I've been out all night, it's 4 A.M. and I just got home. I had snuck some sleeping pills into Brandon's nighttime tea so he wouldn't notice me leave, and it seems to have worked – he's still snoring in his armchair downstairs.

But let's begin with Temple.

I went to a bar in the seedy part of downtown. With no money, no cell phone. Oh, and I was tripping on pills I thought were Vicoprofen but were actually LSD. (Yes, Kurt really is dealing.) But it was a long weird night, let me tell you. The air inside the bar was old, greasy. The furniture was heavy wood, a little dusty. The place smelled vaguely of peanuts.

I made it up to the bar and sat on an empty stool.

The bartender was a smallish, tattooed man. "What would you like?" he asked.

"I just need to use your phone. I'll be happy to pay for some sparkling water, if you have it." I felt on my shoulder for my purse, but it wasn't there. Fuck. Where had I left it? I had to push down panic and get it together. I did not want this to turn into a bad trip. "To be honest, I don't have any money. I must have left my purse in the cab. All I need is a phone so I can call my family." I made my eyes big and imploring.

He peered at me for a few moments, then grabbed the bar's phone and put it on the counter in front of me. I almost cried in relief, and dialed Brandon first. It went straight to voicemail, then told me his mailbox was full. What? He rarely answers his phone in the evening, especially when he's on sleeping pills, but I was hoping that just this once he might. He didn't. I dialed Kurt's number, then remembered the block I had put on the kids' phones. No outside numbers are allowed to call in. I laid my head on the bar and almost let the panic take me over. Then the bartender put a shot in front of me.

"On the house."

"Thank you," I said, and downed it.

I had been there for about half an hour and it felt like the drug was wearing off. I was trying to keep it together, and half-watching the bar patrons by the low, red light on the walls when someone walked in. She was a stately African American wearing a tight, neon-pink dress and 6-inch spiked heels. She glanced around the bar and zeroed in on me. She sauntered over, and I looked down at the remains of my shot.

"Did you take a trip and get lost, honey?" the woman asked.

I nodded.

"Not often we get someone in here that looks like you. I felt you from three blocks over, speed-walked like those white women in malls, all the way here in these damn heels." She laughed.

I had no idea what the woman meant by having 'felt' me. I crossed my legs three different times, I was so nervous.

"Well, are you gonna say anything? What's your name?" Her smile was so warm.

"My name is Joan," I said, and I extended my hand.

"Well hello, Joan. I'm Temple. Pleasure to meet you." She nodded to the bartender and sat on the stool next to me.

Temple told me that she was homeless, a sex worker, and intersexual. "Both parts," she said simply. "I help open people up to their own sexuality. I'm a temple goddess reincarnated."

I smiled. I supposed I'd heard sillier things.

Soon I was telling Temple everything that had happened to me that day, how I was dumb and took from my teenaged son's hand what I thought was Vicoprofen, but ended up being LSD, that I scared the checkout girl at Abercrombie where I was buying Kendra's jeans with my hiding in the clothing rack. How I couldn't even drive, had to catch a cab, and ended up sharing it with a man that I swear was the devil, and who may or may not have stolen my purse.

Head tilted back, eyes closed, nodding at times, Temple was easy to talk to. Because she was listening, really listening. I'm not used to that. Most people in the suburbs listen, smile and nod, but when you pause, they jump right in with an anecdote or remark about themselves.

Then Temple blew my mind.

She said, "See, the difference between you and me, honey, is I'm free. Don't make a mistake thinking I don't have a way of getting myself out of my situation. I do. But I choose not to." She opened her eyes and brought her glass to her lips. "You, on the other hand, you may be living the American Dream, but that dream's gone and a nightmare took its place. The thing you got to understand about yourself, all your friends, family, people in the same tax bracket as you: you're all lost. When you stop living a lie, baby, you start living."

She lit a cigarette, and blew gray circles at the bar ceiling.

"Yeah, Temple, you're absolutely right," I said, shaking my head.

"Temple's gonna set you straight. I can't help you find you, but I can get you closer." She ground her cigarette butt in an ashtray on the bar. "Here's what we gonna do. I'm not your typical homeless prostitute. I have access to all kinds of life-enhancing medicines. You need a bigger experience to set you straight, girl. Do you trust me?"

"Yes," I said, eyes big and trusting. "I do."

It took about an hour for the drug to come on. I hadn't even asked her what the name of it was. I was back to being a teenager.

Her face began to undulate. I heard drums in the back of my head. Was it my own blood, my heartbeat, pounding? Temple grew taller, really tall. I glanced around the bar but now it was a desert. It looked like Arizona, where I grew up. The sun was blazing. Sweat was pouring off me. And Temple was the sun.

We crossed the desert for days. It was so hot and my throat was so dry and I remember Temple dancing and dancing, and I thought she was bringing the rain because she would dance and then bring me a flask of water and help me drink.

Then I doubled over in the sand, coughing and heaving, like an animal was climbing up my windpipe. I couldn't breathe and started to choke. Temple held my hair and stroked my back, like my mother used to when she wasn't yelling. She said, "There, get it all out." I opened my mouth, and a huge ball of wet hair slopped onto the ground.

"It's okay. That's the sickness, honey. Your body's ridding itself of it." Temple patted my back some more. I lay down on the warm sand and sobbed.

§

Temple dropped me off at home. I am dirty, exhausted, but my heart feels strangely light and … happy. It has been so long since I've felt that way.

When she dropped me off I ran to the door. Kendra threw her arms around my neck and Kurt circled his arms around my waist, hugging me from behind. I hugged them tighter than I probably ever have.

With a cup of steaming coffee in front of me, I regaled them with the tale, leaving out the drug bits.

Brandon was still sleeping in his armchair.

After I've got some sleep myself I'll call the cab company, get my purse back, and start making changes. I want to buy new paint supplies, start a class, and do something about this moms' club. Those women need some shaking up, and the new Joan is primed to do it.

Shit. Brandon is coming up the stairs. I think the sleeping pills finally wore off. Until later, diary.

Joan Fixing-My-Shit Colderman

Authors

Rachel Ambrose is a twenty-something fiction writer from Connecticut. Her favorite season is winter, she enjoys well-made Manhattans, and she loves Southern fiction. Her work has appeared in *Crack the Spine, Exiles Literary Magazine*, and *The Colton Review*. Currently at work on her second novel, she blogs at http://victorywhiskeyjuliet.tumblr.com.

Lynn Beighley is a fiction writer stuck in a technical book writer's body. Her stories often involve deeply flawed characters and the unsatisfying meshing of the virtual and actual world. She has an MFA in Creative Writing and currently has 16 books published.

Margaret Bingel is just a writer, living in Manchester, New Hampshire. She spends her time working at her father's beer store, art modeling, and writing (when she can). She doesn't have a website or a blog yet, but who knows, maybe she'll have one in the future.

Guilie Castillo-Oriard is a Mexican writer currently exiled in the island of Curaçao. She misses Mexican food and Mexican *amabilidad*, but the laissez-faire attitude and the beaches of the Caribbean are fair exchange. Plus, the bounty of cultural diversity inspires great culture-clash fiction. Guilie is currently revising and editing her first novel. Her short stories have appeared in *Fiction 365*, *Lady Ink Magazine* and *Pure Slush*. She blogs at http://guilie-castillo-oriard.blogspot.com.

John Wentworth Chapin lives and writes in Baltimore, where he is too frequently starting Project B before finishing Project A. John writes non-fiction as well as fiction. Find him on the web at http://johnwentworthchapin.com.

James Claffey hails from County Westmeath, Ireland, and lives on an avocado ranch in Carpinteria, CA with his family. He is the author of a collection of short fiction, *Blood a Cold Blue*. His website can be found at http://jamesclaffey.com.

Gay Degani has published online and in print including *The Best of Every Day Fiction* editions and her own collection, *Pomegranate Stories*. She is the founder-editor emeritus of EDF's *Flash Fiction Chronicles*, a staff editor at *Smokelong Quarterly*, and blogs at *Words in Place* where a list of her work can be found. She's had two stories nominated for Pushcart consideration and won the eleventh Annual Glass Woman Prize for her flash piece, *Something about L.A.*

Michelle Elvy is an editor and writer who has meandered from the shores of the Chesapeake to New Zealand's Bay of Islands. Michelle has published poetry, short stories and non-fiction about travel, faraway places, food, motorcycling, slow travel, the kindness of strangers and raising children in unusual places for numerous literary journals and magazines in the US, Canada, Australasia, UK and Europe. She edits at *Flash Frontier: An Adventure in Short Fiction* and *Blue Five Notebook*. She can also be found regularly at *Awkword Paper Cut*. More about manuscript assessment and Michelle's take on editing and writing at http://michelleelvy.com.

Gloria Garfunkel is the daughter of two Auschwitz survivors which deeply affected her whole life and personality. She has a Ph.D. from Harvard University in Psychology and Social Relations, concentrating on Personality Development Studies. She was a psychotherapist for thirty years working with children, adults and families. She is currently retired, reading and writing to her heart's content. She has published many stories in journals and anthologies and hopes to eventually publish a collection of her flash fiction. You can find more of her work at her blog http://queruloussquirreldaily.blogspot.com/.

Teresa Burns Gunther has had fiction and nonfiction appear in numerous literary journals and most recently in *Northwind Magazine, Bookslut* and *Best New Writing 2012*. Teresa is the Editor of *The Lakeside*, an on-line literary magazine, and she founded Lakeshore Writers Workshop in Oakland, California where she leads creative writing workshops and classes and works one-on-one with writers. Find her work at http://www.teresaburnsgunther.com/.

Gill Hoffs lives with her family and an ever-dwindling supply of Nutella in the North of England. Find Gill on facebook or as @gillhoffs on twitter, email her a dirty joke at gillhoffs@hotmail.co.uk, or leave a clean comment at http://gillhoffs.wordpress.com/. *Wild: a collection* is out now from *Pure Slush Books*. Her non-fiction book *The Sinking of RMS Tayleur: the Lost Story of the Victorian Titanic* is out now from Pen & Sword. (See her site or http://www.pen-and-sword.co.uk/ for details.) Feel free to send chocolate.

Joanne Jagoda of Oakland, California, took an inspiring writing workshop after retiring in 2009, and launched on a long-postponed creative writing journey. Since discovering her passion for writing, she has worked non-stop on short stories, poetry and non-fiction. Her work has appeared in a number of e-zines and print anthologies, including *Pure Slush* and *Idea Gems Magazine*, and she was a poet of the month for a Jewish news weekly in Northern California. When not taking writing and poetry classes, Joanne enjoys being a writer-coach for ninth graders, Zumba, and visiting her three grandchildren in Jerusalem.

Len Kuntz is a writer from Washington State and an editor at the online literary magazine *Metazen*. His work appears widely in print and online, and you can find him at http://lenkuntz.blogspot.com.

Sally-Anne Macomber was born and raised in Toronto, Canada, and studied journalism at Concordia University in Montreal. Her work on high fashion and the demise of haute couture has appeared in various online and print publications in both Europe and North America. She turned to writing flash fiction in 2010, and hasn't looked back.

Jessica McHugh is an author of speculative fiction that spans the genre from horror and alternate history to epic fantasy. A member of the Horror Writers Association and a 2013 Pulp Ark nominee, she has devoted herself to novels, short stories, poetry, and playwriting. Jessica has had thirteen books published in five years, including the bestselling *Rabbits in the Garden*, *The Sky: The World* and the gritty coming-of-age thriller, *PINS*. More info on her speculations and publications can be found at http://www.jessicamchughbooks.com.

Gwendolyn Joyce Mintz is a fiction writer and aspiring photographer. Her work has appeared in various online and print publications. In other incarnations, Mintz is a writing instructor, a teddy bear maker and somebody's grand-mother.

h. l. nelson is Founding Editor / Executive Director of *Cease, Cows* lit mag and a former sidewalk mannequin. (Yes, that happened.) Pub credits: *PANK, Hobart, Connotation Press, Metazen, Drunk Monkeys, Red Fez, Bartleby Snopes*, blah blah blah. She is working on an anthology, which includes stories by Aimee Bender, Roxane Gay, Lindsay Hunter, and other fierce women writers. h. l.'s MFA is currently kicking her ass. Please tell her what you're wearing here: heather@hlnelson.com

Mandy Nicol grew up in Melbourne, Australia and made a tree change to country Victoria in the mid-nineties – the decade, not her age. She has various animals including a flockette of pet sheep that are thankful for her vegaquarian habits. She writes short stories and loves flash fiction. *Pure Slush* is the first venue to publish her work.

Derek Osborne lives in eastern Pennsylvania. His work has appeared in *Boston Literary Magazine, Bartleby Snopes, Literary Orphans, The Linnet's Wings, Pure Slush* and many others. To read more visit http://gertrudesflat.blogspot.com, or email him at derekosborne1@gmail.com.

Vanessa Weibler Paris lives in Erie, Pa., with a guy, a girl, a boy, a bunny rabbit and a dog. She writes things both real (for work) and pretend (for fun). Her favorite things include hot peppers, bad puns, small-world stories, and tales with a twist at the end.

Gary Percesepe is Associate Editor at *New World Writing* (formerly *Mississippi Review*) and a Contributor at *The Nervous Breakdown*. Author of four books in philosophy, Percesepe's poetry, fiction, essays, and interviews have appeared in *Story Quarterly, N + 1, Salon, Mississippi Review, The Millions, Brevity, PANK, Metazen, The Brooklyner*, and other places. His collection of short stories,

Why I Did the Grocery Girl, is forthcoming from Aqueous Books. His poetry collection *falling* and his flash fiction collection *itch* were published by *Pure Slush Books* in late 2013. He has taught at Saint Louis University, Wittenberg University, and University of Dayton. He lives in Buffalo, New York.

Matt Potter is an Australian-born writer who keeps a part of his psyche in Berlin. Matt has been published in various places online, and he is, rather amazingly, also the founding editor of *Pure Slush*. You can find more of his work at his website: http://mattcpotter.webs.com/.

Darryl Price was born in Kentucky and educated at Thomas More College. A founding member of L. Jack Roth's Yellow Pages Poets, he has published dozens of chapbooks, and his poems have appeared in many journals. He currently edits *Olentangy Review* with his wife Melissa.

Stephen V. Ramey is an American author from New Castle, Pennsylvania. His work has appeared in many places, including *The Doctor TJ Eckleburg Review*, *The Journal of Compressed Creative Arts*, and *A Capella Zoo*. *Glass Animals*, his first collection of (very) short fiction is available from *Pure Slush Books*. Find him and more of his work at http://www.stephenvramey.com.

Shane Simmons is a self-confessed coffee shop writer who believes that regardless of quality, each paragraph penned should be rewarded with sweet treats (cake, muffins, Belgian waffles, etc). London-born, he ran away to Glasgow ten years ago, expanded his waistline and now blogs at http://scribblingsimmons.wordpress.com/.

Kimberlee Smith is a writer whose poetry, essays, fiction, and creative non-fiction have been published in numerous literary journals and anthologies. She was awarded a residency to the Jentel Arts Program in 2013. She lives with her two daughters, two dogs, three cats, two rabbits, and nine chooks on her farm in rural Connecticut. She received her MA in English from the University of Sydney, a certificate in the Creative Writing Program through UCLA, and her BA in Journalism from the University of Southern California. She is enrolled currently in post-graduate studies at Columbia University in New York. She can do a headstand on a trampoline, kill a chook, and make hard cider from the apples in her orchard.

Andrew Stancek was born in Bratislava and saw Russian tanks occupying his homeland. His dreams of circuses and ice cream, flying and lion-taming, miracle and romance have appeared recently in print in *LA Review*, *Windsor Review* and *New Sun Rising: Stories for Japan*. Among the many online publications featuring his work are *Every Day Fiction*, *Gemini Magazine* (Flash Fiction Contest Grand Prize Winner), *fwriction*, *r.kv.r.y. quarterly literary journal*, *Tin House*, *Flash Fiction* Chronicles, *The Linnet's Wings*, *Connotation Press*, *THIS Literary Magazine*, *LA Review*, *Windsor Review*, *Thrice Fiction Magazine*, *New Sun Rising*, and *Pure Slush* online.

Susan Tepper is the author of four published books of fiction and a chapbook of poetry. Her most recent title *The Merrill Diaries* (*Pure Slush Books*, July 2013) is a Novel in Stories that follows a young woman's adventures in love and lust on two continents, spanning a decade. Tepper has received nine Pushcart nominations, and one for the Pulitzer Prize in fiction. You can visit her website here: http://www.susantepper.com.

Nathaniel Tower lives in the Twin Cities with his wife and daughter. After teaching high school English for nine years, he decided to pursue a career in writing / publishing / editing. His fiction has appeared in over two hundred online and print journals. His first collection of fiction, *Nagging Wives, Foolish Husbands*, was released in 2013 through *Martian Lit*. Nathaniel is the founding and managing editor of *Bartleby Snopes Literary Magazine and Press*. You can find out more about Nathaniel at http://nathanieltower.wordpress.com.

Townsend Walker lives in San Francisco. His stories have been published in over fifty literary journals and included in seven anthologies. One story won the SLO NightWriters story contest. Two were nominated for the PEN / O. Henry Award. Four were performed at the New Short Fiction Series in Hollywood. He is associate editor at *Grey Sparrow Journal*. During a career in finance he published three books, on foreign exchange, derivatives and portfolio management. Educated at Georgetown, NYU and Stanford, his website is at http://www.townsendwalker.com.

Michael Webb is continually surprised anyone is interested in what he has to say, and he blogs occasionally at http://innocentsaccidentshints.blogspot.com.

Other volumes in the *2014* series from Pure Slush

Visit the Pure Slush Store:
http://pureslush.webs.com/store.htm

January 2014 Vol. 1
ISBN: 978-1-925101-03-4

February 2014 Vol. 2
ISBN: 978-1-925101-14-0

March 2014 Vol. 3
ISBN: 978-1-925101-17-1

April 2014 Vol. 5
ISBN: 978-1-925101-27-0

June 2014 Vol. 6
ISBN: 978-1-925101-34-8

July 2014 Vol. 7
ISBN: 978-1-925101-37-9

www.ingramcontent.com/pod-product-compliance
Lightning Source LLC
Chambersburg PA
CBHW050822180626
46814CB00004B/1415